To. Mam

from

The Fire and the Flame Series:
Book 2

Azra and the Warriors of the Ruby Shards

by Risaria

Murray the Sea Warrior

Into the Pit, Death and Transformation

Flying with the Dragon

I'm shivering as we fly, I'm not really prepared for this. My hands are numb from clinging onto the harness and my nose is so cold I seriously begin to wonder if it might drop off. I feel cold and scared. I pull my scarf up higher, but that doesn't change much, it can't disguise that I am clinging tight to the back of a dragon. My hands clench the reins so hard that my knuckles turn white. I feel my stomach turning backflips. So far I haven't dared look down to see how high up we are.

Then I give myself a talking to,

'Call yourself a Dragon Keeper? Come on, this is a long trip you might as well learn to enjoy it. Take a look at the view.'

After a few queasy moments I look down. There below me is my homeland getting smaller and smaller. The desert surrounding my home of Set, that on the ground I think of as endless, looks tiny from up here.

Then my heart jumps into my mouth with the realisation – the world does not end at my home kingdom. There are mountains and oceans and vast lands stretching farther than my eye can see! Now I can see for myself that the tales that Granpa Jonas used to tell me, those stories that Gramma used to tell him not to fill my head with. They are true! My heart soars and my nervousness does a somersault into excitement. Here I am, up in the sky with the birds! This is the stuff that dreams are made of!

climates we will pass through – and a compass, the latter is much to Reggie's amusement and an unnecessary weight, she argues. We're travelling light, the food supplies look pitiful for a journey half way around the world – we are going to have to rely on our wits.

I'm making light of it, but I've never left my homeland before and we're setting off on a journey that I have no real idea of where I'm going or what will be at the other end, so I am scared. Part of me is so scared that I really don't want to go – but this way we have some chance of getting the help we need. The alternative doesn't bear thinking about. Vlast and his army are ten times the size of our little underground motley crew. The only thing we have on our side are the Dragons – but these are all new-born, still vulnerable and easy prey for the hardened Dragon Slayers.

We need help from the Old Dragons, those with the wisdom of the ages, if there are any still alive in the world. It's up to me to find them.

The tale I was told, since I was a child, is that we, the kingdom of Set, are the last people on earth – but we have been told so many things that have proved false, and *The Handbook* claims there *are* people beyond our cut-off kingdom. *The Handbook* has proved right so far, no matter how strange I may find what it says.

The migratory birds spent the night before we left arguing over how long and which route is best for us to take, but a lot of their information is second or third hand, along the lines of:

'The Blue Teal Ducks say it takes thirty days minimum.'

'Well, I met a swift who flew from Scotland to Africa in five days.'

'Those swifts eat and sleep on the wing, never mind the sex!

And there's a chorus of tweeting laughter.

Reggie just sits there looking imperturbable saying, 'I'll find it.'

I know her innate knowledge is supposed to be wonderful, but I'm still nervous and I keep checking *The Dragon Keeper's Handbook* when I'm sure she isn't looking.

One thing that it has shown me is a map. It's a very sketchy map, I don't like the look of it at all, but it's really all I've got to guide us on this journey out of my desert homeland, across what looks like a whole world of what the map simply calls *'Vast Ocean'*.

At least I know where we are headed – Scotland, our ancestral home. Reggie is descended from the green Caledonian dragons. These dragons are so ancient and mythical that their existence has always been disputed.

Other Albion countries, of which Scotland is one, honoured the dragon in their myths and banners – but only the red dragons. The green dragons are said to have been in disgrace, for what it is unclear. All that *The Dragon Keeper's Handbook* has to say on the matter is that the green dragons of Scotland are as old as the earth and they are as wise as they are old.

This is certainly true of Reggie – bonded to me at birth as I was the first living thing that she saw; I'm the nearest thing she has to a parent. Fortunately she has such an innate knowledge I find it staggering what she comes up with – I think this is why she is so offended by the compass – she just *knows* the way home to Scotland.

This would work if I was more trusting but I'm not. Reggie is an optimist, which is great ninety per cent of the time, but on a journey like this when she keeps saying, 'We don't need a map, just trust me,' – well, if I could throttle her serpentine scaly neck I would.

Before we left Set, *The Dragon Keeper's Handbook* took Reggie's remarks about the map and the compass as an insult and went into a sulk for three days, telling me that we didn't appreciate it. It hid itself as a shoe –

words they use. Also when someone is good and loves you.

I tell her this.

'Yes. I know that feeling. But this is more...You start off *hoping* something. Like when I was hoping we would make this trip. Then it became positive, I just expected it was going to happen. But really, all along I *knew* we were going to do this. I felt it in my bones.'

'Me too!' I exclaim.

So I breathe – and say out loud, 'I enjoy flying with Reggie.'

That doesn't even come close to what I feel. I sing out at the top of my voice 'I *love* flying with you, Reggie!' My voice sings out in the clear air, my insides leap – this time with joy – and my heart starts singing.

It's exhilarating, I feel alive and breathe in the cool refreshing air, my head is buzzing with excitement!

Way, way down below us I spot something in the water. I point it out to Reggie and she loops down for a closer look. 'What are they?' I ask out loud.

'School of bottlenose dolphins; pod of 8 adults four young.' Is The Handbook's immediate response.

'How can you know this?' I ask in amazement. 'If your knowledge comes from Dragon Keepers who are now dead how can you know what they are below us?'

'...Because every Dragon Keeper is still connected to me. My knowledge is as old as the Dragon Keepers. For example, the Dragon Keeper who is the most knowledgeable about the oceans and has written a really great chapter on the wildlife, when you ask a question about them it instantly connects with them and the information is updated.'

I'm not sure if I get all that, what I do know is that, swimming below us are these amazingly beautiful creatures – leaping and diving. They spot us and start calling to each other whistling, chirping and screaming. They leap into the air and Reggie dives down playfully and they circle round us. They seem very excited to see us. One, the oldest and largest, leaps and dips as if bowing to us. Reggie bows in return. 'I wish I knew what they were saying.'

Instantly *The Handbook* turns a page and I read its reply,

'They are welcoming you. They are pleased to see that the dragons are back on the move. They are surprised at seeing one so young riding a dragon. The old one pays her respects as she is delighted and honoured to be alive to see the stories come true.'

'Stories, what stories?' I ask.

'The stories that tell of a young girl riding on a dragon, for then magic will return to the earth.'

I don't want to ask more, I feel a little fearful. It reminds me of my mother's last words: 'You have to live for all our sakes; you have to bring the dragons back.'

I don't know what they expect of me. I've no idea what this is about but I can feel the fear that I might not be able to do what is expected of me.

'Cheer up!' Reggie says suddenly. 'You've gone all quiet. Stop reading that book and enjoy the view.'

She's right – we are in a glorious bright blue sky with the vast shades of the ocean below – blue, green, aqua and the dolphin's calls have brought others. A whale surprises us as it breaches the water ahead of us, spouting air as it reaches the surface.

Reggie rears in surprise and I clutch desperately at the safety reins to stay astride her. I had relaxed my grip, feeling confident in my balance and safe within the pocket of air created between her wings;

'Stop! We must stop.'

'No, it's too dangerous. We will stop where we can find food and when we need rest, but we are not making contact.' Reggie is adamant. 'We have a job to do.'

'But this proves that it was a lie, there is still life outside Set.'

'Those are just houses.'

'That is more than just houses, it's a *city*.' As a gaze even more intently I see movement, 'I can see *people!* Oh look there are cars *moving without horses*!'

I pause taking in the enormity of this.

I had grown up with horse drawn cars. Our horse Rufus was so beautiful and loveable, a loyal massive creature. Granpa told me that in his youth they didn't need horses to pull the cars as they had what he called an internal combustion engine. This was driven by fire and hidden under the hood of the car. I gaze down at the cars in the streets below, not a horse in sight.

'They must have fire.'

'Everyone has fire, it is only a fool like King Qahir who bans fire from a land,' Regnatha retorts. She is still flying, in a direct line to the west.

'Yes we could stop and meet people. Remember what our experience of people has been?'

'There are good people, Reggie, look how many good people we know...' I falter and remember that she doesn't really know the people that I know and my heart sinks as I wonder if Granpa Jonas is still alive.

She must sense how down I feel for she tries to console me.

'That will take time, Azra, it will delay us if we stop and get to know people. This way we get to Scotland quicker and when we are finished I am sure that, one day, we can visit these lands.'

I know she is right, but it doesn't stop me gazing in longing at the people in the streets. I think she can feel the strength of my desire.

'I will bring you back, one day. I promise.' But she does not know that that is a promise that she will not be able to keep.

I gaze longingly in silence at the changing scene below, Reggie has turned and gained height to avoid us being seen over the city and now we are flying over dense foliage, she flies lower and we see a vast forest stretching for hundreds of miles, no trace of roads, only a river running through it. In the end she gives a sigh and slows down.

'All right. We'll take a *short* pause. We can find some food – but that is all.'

The lush forest is full of trees laden with ripe fruit, fruit that looks like it hasn't been gathered for years. We sit atop the trees picking and eating to our hearts content. There are apes gibbering in the distance – and an image of my father flashes into my mind. I don't remember how old I was, I am sitting on the ground and he is jumping around pretending to be a monkey –

making sounds just as these apes are. He gets me to follow him and we slope around, knuckles on the ground, into the room where my mother sits reading. My ape father knocks the book flying from her hands and motions with his head and gibbering noises to come and join us. She starts laughing uncontrollably, as my father tickles her and rolls her onto the floor. We jump and gibber around her. In between her gulps of laughter she blurts out to us,

'Do you know,' chortle, chortle, 'that a group of apes is called a *shrewdness*.'

My father tickles her with his ape arms, '*Shrewdness? Shrewdness?*' he says in his monkey voice. '

It's so clear this memory and I pause midbite and mimic the apes: 'Shrewdness. Shrewdness.' I feel a warm glow – I didn't know I had this memory inside me and it feels like my heart has come to life, my past isn't just a dark tale there is love in it and fun. I want to savour it even more.

I stand on the branch gibbering and telling Reggie the story in strange bursts.

By now my belly is swollen with the luscious fruit and make wonderful gurgling noises, I laugh and as I turn to Reggie I see she is swaying. 'Careful,' I tell her, 'You look like Granpa when he's had too much of his medicine.'

I hiccup and it isn't just Reggie swaying, it's me!

I realise this too late. As I sway in the treetop I see Reggie as if in slow motion reach out to me, but she too is moving strangely and giggling a hiccupy dragon giggle and gives a belch of fire that smells like rotten eggs. I fall from the tree, catching on twigs and leaves and branches as I tumble.

As I fall I hold my arms up to reach out to Reggie calling, 'I looooooove yooo-uuu' and it echoes around the forest – until all else is silent.

It reminds me of my Granpa Jonas when he had too much medicine, Gramma would scold him and say he was drunk. 'I think I'm drunk.' I hiccup as I land in beautifully soft squishy pile of very soft, very smelly fermenting fruit.

For some moments the forest is still and silent – then I see I am surrounded by curious apes and birds.

'Time to go' says Reggie.

She picks me up in her teeth, up over the treetops until we come to the stream. She dumps me in the water and remains at the water's edge drinking copiously. As I splutter to the surface I hear shouts.

'Look, a girl!'

Reggie hears too. We both freeze, but I see she is camouflaged among the rocks and trees. I motion her to stay.

It's one thing a strange girl but a dragon is quite another.

Two boys paddle towards me – and I swim to meet them, leading them away from Reggie. They both carry small spears. They are brown, very brown skinned with straight hair and white teeth. They wear a strip of cloth to cover their privates – and that is all. They offer their hands to pull me into the boat.

'A white girl,' they say to each other.

'I'm not white' I protest. I look at my brown arms and compare them to their dark almost black bodies. I suppose to them I am - my mix of Settler and Scottish means I am not white enough to be Scottish and not dark enough to be Settler. I shake my wet hair, spraying them with water. I apologise, but they just laugh.

'Where are you from?' They ask.

I have no trouble understanding their language. Their accents are strong, but the tongue is the same as mine.

I point vaguely eastwards. I am holding onto their boat to steady myself.

'Come with us,' they seize my hands and pull me on board, I try and resist but all I can do is giggle and fall.

'She is fruit-drunk,' one of them declares.

I hear a low rumbling a sound that I haven't heard before, but I know must be

Reggie. The boys hear it too and glance at each other fearfully.

'Go.' I say. 'I'm fine. She's with me.'

'Who?' but the words freeze on their lips and I see their eyes focus behind me and their jaws drop.

'Go!' I repeat.

There is no need to repeat it – they have both dived off the boat as Reggie lands on it, her weight tipping it below the water

'Come,' is all Reggie says, but I feel the displeasure behind the word. That one word sobers me instantly.

'I'm sorry. You were right.' I tell her as I climb up and tie myself into my harness.

'We need to be more careful. They were no threat but...'

'You're right, they weren't. We were lucky - this time.'

Reggie snorts.

'Just because they are different to us, different clothes, different habits, doesn't mean that they aren't friendly.'

She ignores me, but it doesn't stop me. I chatter on telling her my theories and philosophies – but I don't get a response from her.

That night when we land I confront her. 'You can't sulk just because I made a mistake.'

She scratches at the earth with her right claw, making great grooves, then pushes the soil back into the furrows.

'We have a long way to go. I don't know how I know that, but I do. And I am afraid for you, Azra. I'm not afraid for myself. I feel I need to keep you safe and for me to do that I need to keep you away from people.'

I pet her gently behind her ear, where the scales are softer. She likes it and nuzzles in towards me.

'All right, I agree. No more people until we reach Scotland.'

I don't want to go to sleep like this, feeling that I've done something wrong. I want to feel better than this.

'You must admit that fruit was really delicious.'

She nods in agreement.

I gather twigs and create a fire – such an easy natural thing to do for me now, yet for the first sixteen years of my life I had no idea what fire or hot food was. Fire was banned in Set after my aunt foretold that Prince Samardashee would destroy both the King and the kingdom with fire.

'Those boys were quite helpful,' I say, conversationally, then I realise that I'm pushing her a little too far.

'It all worked out in the end.' She lays her head on her paws with a sigh.

I remember the memory of my father and mother and how it felt, so I tell Reggie the story and she smiles, for this is something she can understand, to have a good feeling memory of the past.

I would not have been so relieved if I had known what was in store!

When Fire and Ice meet

Years later I read *The Handbook's* retelling of our journey – for it too recorded its own view of the stories of the Dragon Keepers, although fortunately for me I did not realise this for many years. It told a tale of the bravery of a young girl and her dragon. I didn't recognise myself for it talked of a bravery that I didn't feel at the time. There was no time to think of being brave – when you are facing the elements you do not think, you have to focus. Focus on what is the next best thing to do, when the storms whip the sea into a frenzy, when there is nothing to eat and Reggie is exhausted.

The first time a storm hit us Reggie found an island that was barely more than a rock in the ocean. We took shelter beneath an overhanging ledge. I was wet and shivering and shuddering with fear – it was a terrific storm.

Reggie looked at me and said, 'We need a fire – if only we could burn that *Handbook*!'

'I'd love a fire more than anything.'

To our amazement *The Handbook* sprang open and its blank pages began tearing themselves out and crumpling up into a ball. Then a picture appeared in the book, we watched intently as it grew – first one tree then more and more, until a whole forest grew up on the page branches fell and twigs jumped from the pages onto the crumpled paper. As it came to a stop Reggie turned and after some coughing, was able to muster a smoky damp breath with just enough flame to ignite the fire.

I dried my hair and warmed my hands at the flames as I read what *The Handbook* revealed to me:

'Whatsoever emotion you feel or any thought that you think it will attract more to itself. Thoughts and feelings act like magnets. Be aware of what you are thinking and if it is what you wish to attract then think and feel more of it. If is what you do not wish to attract, then change your thoughts to what you do desire.'

As I read I remembered my mother saying something like this to me. I smiled at her memory and stroked the words, for they could be her very words.

The fire flared up, forming a picture of her within it – the blue flame the colour of her favourite gown. Her hand reached out to me and I heard her voice, or maybe it was just the memory of it, saying:

'Always focus on your heart's desire, my darling. It's no use dwelling on the past and what might have been. What will make you happy – that is all you need to think of.'

'So its like being granted a wish.'

'Just like that. The real magic is in the knowing inside you, the knowing that comes from there is much stronger and more powerful than any knowledge you can gain from elsewhere. If you appreciate things rather than be fearful of them then everything is transformed.'

That night I learnt that if I felt fearful it was no help whatsoever – I had been cowering fearfully, too scared to look out at what was going on around me.

So I decided that I wanted to be surrounded by beautiful things and as I watched the massive bolts of lightning and sheets of rain I began admiring their beauty. The more I saw them as beautiful the more awesome they appeared to me. As any fear dissolved my feelings changed to wonder at their magnificence. Then it seemed that they were now at a safer distance, where I could appreciate them more

From then on I reminded myself of where we were headed and focused on the practicalities of each step: finding a safe place for the night, finding food to eat, checking we were heading in the right direction – though that was straightforward as Reggie's inbuilt compass was directing her to her ancestral home. As I did this then fears just became background noise.

Some days we played games. *'I Spy'* was the most challenging, especially when you are surrounded by sun, sea and sky and decide that we couldn't use the letter '*s*' any more.

'The Rain Game' was one of my favourites. The challenge was to find the end of the raincloud and Reggie would hover, so I could have one hand held out into the rain, the other hand outstretched in the sun.

'*Counting Rainbows*' was another favourite. The first time I saw a full rainbow I could not believe it – a complete circle of red, orange, yellow, green, blue, indigo and violet. My mouth must have been as round as the rainbow. I asked Reggie to stop and she hovered while I stared open-mouthed at the beauty of the colours reflected on the clouds. *The Handbook* told me that all rainbows are circles, it's just that when we see them from the ground the horizon cuts off the circle, making the rainbow look like an arc.

It also told of other amazing things to look out for: *moonbows* created by the moonlight – more delicate in colour than rainbows which are created by the sun and hauntingly beautiful in the night sky. We also discovered *Glories* – when our own shadows are reflected onto a cloud surrounded by a halo of coloured light. At the sight of a *Glory* Reggie and I stayed until the cloud shifted and the image was lost, so beautiful was this sight. These were rare opportunities that were great to experience and such fun, yet my favourite game of all was the one I was able to play most days – *Cloud Spotting*.

In the desert I was so used to clear blue skies – and for most of my life my view of the world was the sky above my rooftop bed. I was used to clear skies and to painting the colours of the sky, to drawing the patterns of the stars, but out here the clouds fascinated me. *The Dragon Keeper's Handbook* gave me the names for them all, each new one that I found I felt a great fillip inside me and when I flew through one for the first time! Wow! The feeling of the moisture on my skin, the strange quality to the air that we were breathing in made me feel exhilarated and giddy. And the silence – the silence was so calming and still that after my initial fears on my first flight I never again had a fear of falling, it was like being out of time up here.

These experiences I saw as gifts and they began to appear, I decided, to inspire us and keep us focused on our journey. Then when we had our *Wake Up Call* I realised that it was as if I had a hand in creating these experiences too.

In the evenings I read to Reggie from *The Dragon Keeper's Handbook*. She still had not much time for *The Handbook* – though she did admit it was good for making fires! However, she liked listening when I read stories of dragons from it.

She was particularly scathing one evening when, instead of a story, *The Handbook* had three pages of practical tips on *'How To Fall'*.

'What a waste of magic!' she snorted.

I was disappointed myself, but *The Handbook* would only reveal what it felt you were ready to know and would refuse to turn to another page. So if it thought this was important then I supposed I had better read it. I told Reggie to find something better to do as I wanted to read – but in reality, I mainly just looked at the pictures.

The day of our *Wake-Up Call* dawned and we were both disgruntled, I started asking how much farther we had to fly and this set Reggie off.

'How am I supposed to know? This is my first time too. I may have inbuilt navigational skills, but it doesn't come with a mileometer.'

I'd really upset her, I tried to bring her out of it, but she refused to play any games.

'I've got more important things to do than cloud spotting – you just lie back and have fun.' She almost spat the word *fun* at me, so I let her be.

I didn't blame her really, we had flown for hundreds of miles over seemingly endless tracts of sea. I was the one able to just sit back and fall asleep as the heat of the sun beat down. Reggie was the one doing all the work. I felt so safe with her and trusted her completely. Now I didn't bother strapping in unless the weather looked stormy.

I began singing – usually a sure certainty to raise her spirits – but she would have none of it and snapped at me to turn the volume down. After some hours of trying to entertain myself – it wasn't the same without her excitement to share when one of us spots a particularly unusual cloud – I fall asleep.

I wake to a roaring squawk from Reggie – so strong and urgent that the vibration of it courses through her body and sets me trembling – as she screams the words 'Strap in.'

By now it is dark and we are in cloud, but these clouds are unlike any I have ever seen before. They are thin trailing wisps, like the tailcoats of ghosts. The air is bitingly cold. I shudder. There is no land below us only the dark sea and it is so cold and turbulent I know that Regnatha won't want to land on it.

Ahead of us through a break in the wisps of clouds there is a dark mass that might be land. We fly towards it as the clouds merge and hide it from view. 'Hold on,' calls Regnatha as she takes us onto the swirling mass of wisping cloud to ride the air currents that are looping towards land.

The wind is biting cold and in the moment when my hood falls off it feels like my nose and ears are turning to icicles and my hair into icy frosting. My brain is freezing too. I pull Samardashee's cloak tight around me, then I forget the cold, I forget everything at the sight unfolding before me.

The clouds are changing colours and shapes. There is a glorious silence – yet it feels full of sound. Great waves of green, an intense green that is brighter than anything I have ever seen before. These waves like cosmic curtains fold and unfurl across the sky. Then they part and a great wave of purple blue passes overhead. I feel like I am swimming in the sky. With giddy delight we ride these massive swirling currents and just as I felt I was about to pass out a huge deep, deep purple-blue-red blanket covered in stars, like the one my Gramma had made me, fills the sky.

I am so awed by this that when Regnatha suddenly screams I am taken completely unawares. I've been looking above us, but she is focused ahead and there dead in front of us is a dragon. But what a dragon!

This dragon is looming up, so huge it fills the sky. It's bright green head opens wide, engulfing us as it swoops down. Regnatha falls. We are falling, falling so fast, and I am upside down with Regnatha's unconscious body on top of me. Suddenly I react, my brain kicks into instinctive mode, I know if we hit the water like this I will be killed on impact.

My freezing, trembling fingers unbuckle the straps as we fall through the icy air. As I pull free I haul myself up to Reggie's neck. I pull up one eyelid – her blank eyeball confirms what I already know, she is unconscious. I blow into it, it is all I can think of doing, no response.

Then I remember being hit – but not by the storm. I have the impression of a raptor like creature with pointed head, wings and claws tearing into us.

I tumble from my perch on Reggie down through the storm clouds Tumbling and turning through space, everything is in slow motion, but my mind has stopped, by the time I can think what to do my rain-soaked cloak wraps itself around me trapping my arms and legs. I see above me on my slow turn through space the tiny, angular shape of a dragon silhouetted against the bright green sky dragon. Then I hear Reggie scream and I think, 'Ah good, she's alive!' As I fall everything fades as, strange as it may seem, I start to enjoy the sensation of falling. There is nothing I can do but to let go.

Suddenly I hear *The Handbook*. I had not consciously remembered it but as I fell it was as if my mind flicked open at the pages I had read last night on '*How to Fall'* and a voice, or rather the information was suddenly there – I *knew* what to do.

So I did it.

My arms were pinioned at my side by the strait-jacket of my rain-sodden cloak, but this is a bonus. I arch my back to slow my speed. I check below for the best spot to land, then pull my left shoulder down to steer away from a rock in the sea below. My speed has accelerated and now I'm falling – fast. I point my toes as I enter the water feet first. The impact is tremendous and I plunge so deep into the waters that my whole body is bursting and screaming for air.

That is all that I remember before passing out.

I come around slowly, before I open my eyes I feel tiny grains of sand beneath my fingertips. They remind me of home. I feel a flood of gratitude sweep through me as I draw breath and realise - I am alive!

Then the memory of what happened floods back, startled I open my salt encrusted eyes. Where am I?

Above me is a massive rock wall as far as I can see, with ferns and plants growing all over it. There is the sound of running water, I turn my head towards it and see a waterfall cascading a hundred feet or more into a rock pool. It's a beautiful sight.

Then my gaze falls onto Reggie lying beside me. She is blue, but not the glorious blue I know and love, this is a grey blue, as if the life blood has drained out of her. I try to speak her name, but I can hardly breathe, my lungs feel as if they had been crushed.

'Let her sleep child she needs to rest and so do you.'

The voice comes from the gloom at my feet.

At first all I can see is two rheumy grey eyes. Then my gaze expands and I see this is a vast, ancient creature. It moves towards me, its grey scales billowing dust at every step. This is a dragon, but what a dragon – it seems older than the rocks that shelter us and if dragons grow at each and every trial they experience then this one has been to hell and back.

This is not the green sky dragon of last night, this dragon has lost all colour, as if it has faded to this dusty grey. I do not feel in fear of attack, but I still gasp in surprise at the size of this immense creature – then wince at the pain of breathing.

'Be still. You are not broken but your body needs to rest.'

I glance across at Reggie and the old dragon notices.

He does not answer my unspoken question.

'Is she...' I hesitate' choosing my words carefully for I so want this to be true, 'Is she alive?'

'Och aye. It would take more than that to destroy a dragon like her. What is her name?'

'Reg... Regnatha'

'A beautiful name for a beautiful dragon. Regnatha.'

The way he says it he rolls the *R* around his mouth and the sound reverberates around the cavern I feel it shivering through the rock beneath me, its vibration rippling throughout the earth and it resounds in Reggie. She stirs her and her eyes open.

'Reggie!' I sit up, excited.

'You're alive!' Reggie and I chorus together – but I'm shocked at the weakness of her voice.

The old dragon gazes at me intently, a gaze that I feel sees into my very soul.

'You are bonded!' he declaims.

He says this with great surprise then mutters to himself, 'Of course, you would have to be for her to let you harness her like that.'

He moves to add more fuel to a fire he has burning beside us. He scoops a huge cauldron up in his left claw and fills it at the waterfall and puts it on the fire – as he moves around there is the sound of a great chain dragging along the rock floor. The sound disturbs me more than anything else in this strange place, but I cannot see where it is coming from.

'Are we prisoners?' I ask.

'Hush child, you aren't prisoners. You're safe here, just rest."

So I lay there going over the events of the day that had brought us here. With hindsight I see that how Reggie and I had started each morning affected the whole day.

When we were excited and frisky, enjoying the sheer delight of skimming over the ocean or sailing through the sky the journey was at its most joyful – sheer pleasure. But that day, after a night of being plain stubborn and miserable, we started the day being – what I learn later that the Scots call – *crabbit*. First, I complained about fish for breakfast, again, I complained about the weather being too misty and damp.

'And yesterday was too hot and dry for you! There is no pleasing you,' Reggie announced. 'Well,' she said, 'Me being as miserable as you won't help at all. I can't cheer you up but at least I can make myself happy.' Saying this, to my amazement, she began to sing!

As we took off she sang out about all the beauty in the world around us. She sang of the bright blue sky with wisps of cloud to shade us. She sang a song of her delight at the ocean, a patchwork of shifting colours of the turquoise and aquamarine, of the dark mystery of its depths. She sang of her joy at how it mirrored the brilliant sunlight, creating a pathway that seemed to guide us. She even sang of how our shadows on the clouds were our companions along the way. *The Handbook* had told me that there were great mountains and even ancient cities under the oceans. On any other day this was enough to send me off into a world of wonder, imagining how I would explore those great depths. On this day I was so darned miserable I pulled my cloak over me and stuffed my ears to keep out her darned cheerfulness. In my dark cocoon all

I wanted to do was to get *there* – wherever *there* may be.

If there were any justice in this world, I thought to myself, it would be me, miserable me, with a severed arm.

Why Reggie, why not me?

That was the question that ran through my mind as I lay there beside my beloved Reggie.

As I asked this a voice said, 'You got what you asked for.'

'What?!' I cry out aloud, 'I didn't ask to be attacked.'

'Hush child,' the old dragon soothed me. 'You are dreaming.'

I wait until he turns his back.

I wasn't dreaming, the voice came from under my head, not in it. I pull out the backpack pillow that my head is resting on and immediately *The Handbook* starts to shape shift to its part book part rock state.

I whisper so as not to disturb the old dragon – it feels important to keep *The Handbook* to myself for now. 'Are you talking to me?' I ask it.

Its voice sounds like rustling pages.

'*Of course!* Who else could I be talking to? You are the only one who can hear us!'

I breathe a sigh of relief and realise that it's only when *I* talk that the dragon can hear.

It wriggles so much in my tight grasp that I drop it and it heaves a great dusty sigh of relief that sets me coughing.

'You have to let us breathe when we are transforming, it's incredibly difficult to shape shift at the best of times.'

'What do you mean – I *asked* for what happened?' I demand as loudly as I dare.

The Handbook gives a deep sigh.

'You wanted to get *there*. So now you are *there* – the end, your destination.'

'Not like this! I meant for us to get here in one piece, safely.' My voice is so shrill it echoes around the cavern. The vast dragon turns towards me and Regnatha stirs.

'I'm sorry,' I say, and he holds my gaze for some moments to ensure that I remain quiet as he places a wing tenderly onto Reggie to reassure her.

The Handbook bangs its covers together with a loud slap that I am sure will make the dragon turn, but it does not.

'You attracted the same vibration that you were giving out.' it tells me.

'What is that supposed to mean?' I asked.

'You were impatient and wanted the journey to end and get to your destination. So here you are in Scotland.

'Scotland! We're in Scotland?'

Reggie groans and the old dragon turns to me with a snort.

'Aye, lassie and I beg you to be more quiet,' he tells me.

At that I have an idea that I think will work. I pull my cloak over myself and *The Handbook* creating a den for us to talk in. Under it my voice is soundproofed.

'But what about Reggie I ask? She was trying to cheer me up, she was happy.'

'Ah, yes, that's as may be.' *The Handbook* continues. 'The thing with

Regnatha is that she too had had enough – she wanted to stop flying.'

It came back to me then as I remembered our conversation that morning as she prepared breakfast – we were grumbling at each other and as I was telling her to hurry up she turned to me and said, 'If I never fly again I'd be happy.'

'Do you mean she won't be able to fly again? She didn't mean it like that, that is such a terrible thing to do – did you do that? That is just cruel.'

I lower the cloak and a lump comes into my throat as I look at Reggie there beside me, her wing lying limp and useless. I notice that there is a row of green crystals laid out along it marking the dividing line between the pulsing and severed muscles.

'Her wing tendons are severed and there is poison in the wound,' says a voice like tinkling water. Startled I look around, it isn't the old dragon – who is this? I can't see anyone; the voice seems to be coming from a spot of light in a corner where no sunlight could possibly reach.

Reggie opens her eyes and asks, 'Azra?'

'Here,' I manage to choke out, relieved at hearing her.

I reach out towards her and though my fingers cannot touch her, it's as if she feels me.

She turns her loving gaze on me and my heart skips a beat as I feel her love for me and mine for her.

'Will I fly again?'

Once again there is the sound of rusty chains and rattling as the old dragon turns uncomfortably. He shakes his head and reluctantly says, 'It is too soon to say.' His words belie his true feelings, his fear that she may not. And Azra can see his emotions come from a great depth as if travelling from a place that has not been touched in many, many years these words so full of tenderness.

'I'm sorry, I have failed you, Azra,' she says to me.

I see a great translucent globe roll and fall from her eye, it rolls towards me and I see my own reflection in it, I feel it, wet against my ear – a teardrop. First singly then more rapidly they flow from Reggie's beautiful green eyes in a rivulet across the cave floor towards me. Then I hear a sound of tinkling bells and a flash of light – or *some thing* – flashes past me and rapidly scoops up the tears into a glass phial.

'You have not failed you have brought her here safely to Scotland, Regnatha.' The tinkling voice hovers around Regnatha's head, soothing her brow.

'Her main wish was to protect *you*, child, and that she has done well,' says the tinkling voice.

Sometimes when you are in a dark place you think you will never get out. I learnt that when I was hidden in the chimney watching my mother die. It is the sort of thing that you think you can never live through, that you will never get over. But you do, you have to or else you aren't living you are just suffering. My Granpa Jonas taught me that it was okay to have fun again, that it was important that I did for my own sake, my mother would not have wanted me to live an unhappy life. He told me it was okay to laugh – and I did because my beautiful mother had given her life for me and so I wanted to make the most of it. I didn't want to waste my life by being miserable. So Granpa taught me to juggle. Juggling helped me learn to be happy again – when you are juggling you have to focus, you cannot take your eye off the ball. Juggling has helped me a lot – and when I thought I was going to lose Regnatha it came to my rescue in a totally unexpected way.

The '*some thing*' that had flashed by me to scoop up Regnatha's tears revealed itself as the strangest creature I have ever seen. Her skin, I was sure she was female, was a delicate shade of green that changed with the light. Her hair was blonde yet also appeared green as it caught the light. At least it did when she was visible, sometimes she moved so fast she was invisible and the only sign of her was a passing breeze or – if you were sharp-eyed enough – a glimpse of green.

The creature stood still to bottle the tears and etch a label into the glass with her delicately pointed nails.

'She will live,' the old dragon declares, 'If this elf here says so then I know it will be so.'

'An elf?' I say, and hearing the incredulity in my own voice I think to myself, *'You should know better by now – you're here with a dragon,'*

The elf laughs – a sound like tinkling water, 'I am Tracy and I am only part elf, my grandmother was human and this here – for I am sure he will never get around to telling you his name, is Astarot, the most ancient dragon on the planet.'

Tracy holds out a hand so slender and cool it feels to me like I am dipping my hand into a cool mountain stream. Just to touch her is refreshing.

'I'm Azra,' I pause knowing I should say more but all I can think of is, 'I'm from the kingdom of Set.'

'Are you pure human, Azra?' she asks. I nod.

'There is something about you... And for a *human* to be bonded to a dragon is, well, rare to say the least.'

'My parents are... were Dragon Keepers,' I admit. My mistake makes me realize that it is my conversations with *The Dragon Keeper's Handbook* that make me feel more and more that my parents are still with me. Then a thought flashes into my mind – maybe it isn't a mistake, maybe they are?

'As are you?'

I say 'Yes' before the thought 'Is it safe to admit this?' comes to me.

I have only known that I was a Dragon Keeper for less than a year, since my sixteenth birthday. All my life it has been dangerous to even know a Dragon Keeper, never mind be related to one. It was believed that the Dragon Slayers had killed all the Dragon Keepers and I've been so used to keeping the secret my whole life that I'm shocked to hear myself tell her so readily.

I want to change the subject, so I ask, 'What are you going to do with them?' as she carefully stores the phial of Reggie's tears in her woven bag.

'Dragons' tears have great healing power and magic in them. It's important not to waste these gifts, it is a rare occasion when a dragon cries. Thankfully,' she adds.

'Why thankfully?'

'Because their sorrow reverberates throughout the world.' She looks closely at me as she explains, 'When a dragon cries there is a tsunami on the other side of the planet.'

I shiver.

She sees my reaction and tempers her comment. 'Fortunately, by catching them as they fall it lessens the impact.'

'How?' I ask.

'They don't soak into the earth, so their energy is contained.' She holds the phial up for me to see.

'However, there is still some of it about. We are all connected. This...' she waves her hands around the spacious cavern and I look to see what she is gesturing at.

As she moves her fingers the air sparkles and tinkles and falls on me waving through my hair like a summer's breeze but with a hint of moisture from Regnatha's tears in it that suddenly makes me feel sad.

'This stuff you call air carries all our emotions: the laughter, the sorrow, whatever – and it creates waves, ripples in the vibration.'

She moves her hand swiftly through the air and I feel tears well up inside me.

'See how you feel even sadder? That is the dragon's sorrow vibrating through the matrix, air, *stuff* whatever you want to call it.'

'What do you call it?' I ask her.

'I call it magic – it is the miracle whence dreams become real, our inner knowing. It is how we communicate with each other without words. That is why it is important not to waste a dragon's tears – for while they contain sorrow they also contain relief, they can release and let go old ills and patterns.'

Gently she takes one of Regnatha's tears from the phial. As it catches the light I think I see a swirl of faces – my father, my mother, my Gramma. Did I see Granpa Jonas? My heart leaps into my mouth at the sight – fleeting glimpses of them looking worriedly at me and I wonder if Granpa is all right, is he still alive? The images disappear, lost as she wipes my face with the tear, washing me gently, stroking my brow, my cheeks, my chin and as she does the sorrow pours away – taking with it a sadness, a longing that I hadn't realized I have been carrying with me for most of my life. I feel lighter, like a weight is lifted from me and my face and skin feel fresh and alive.

She kisses me on the nose and magics three juggling balls out of thin air. She tosses them in the air then throws them to me – instinctively I catch them and to my surprise and delight I am juggling effortlessly.

I am transported back to the days I had forgotten, when happiness seemed never-ending. As the balls turn and change mid-air I feel I am playing with my mother and father and we juggle and laugh together. My heart lightens and as I laugh the old sad images of my past disappear and the happy days, the fun times come to the forefront. I am seeing my old story in a new light.

Then Tracy takes over the balls and the images of the past disappear and I am right here, right now with these new friends – and even Regnatha is smiling!

From that moment I know Tracy and I will be friends forever. This moment alone would have been enough but the fact that she is an elf *and* she has saved Regnatha's life – well, that just makes it inevitable.

Tracy disappears the juggling balls into her bag, 'Yes,' she says, 'Laughter really is the best medicine.'

I wake to the sound of water, rain is pouring in the cave and there is a dim light which must mean it is dawn. I am lying huddled up to Reggie's back where I have crawled to be closer to her. The potion that Tracy has given her has done its work, she is in a deep sleep, her breathing low and steady, snoring peacefully.

Now that I am rested I am full of questions

'We are in Scotland.' I say out loud, 'How can that be when I thought we were miles away.'

'Distance is a funny thing lassie. Often we are closer to home than we realize.' I turn to Astarot's voice.

At that moment a vast shadow passes over the light and there silhouetted against the morning sun is a shape – the same raptor shape of last night – swoops into the cave towards Reggie.

'You!' I'm on my feet and leap between the creature and Regnatha with nothing but my hands and feet to defend her. My speed surprises us all. I kick the thing dead centre in the belly. My surprise attack hurls it through the air. It does nothing to retaliate, merely recovers itself and lands at a safe distance from me, slightly behind Astarot. This surprises me and my adrenalin rush subsides and I realize that the massive shadow has deceived me, this creature is so much smaller than it seemed last night.

Something flashes before me and dizzy and weak I fall backwards. A dazzling light hovers over me – Tracy.

'Stop!' The tinkling voice shrills. 'He saved her!'

I lie there helpless, panting from the adrenalin rush that launched me into action to protect Reggie. I see blood dripping from the little creature's nostril and tears from its eyes. Now that I get a closer look it looks incredibly small and in daylight it seems quite harmless.

Tracy is still now and I watch her tend the injured creature – only after he nods that he is okay does she bring out her phials to collect the blood and tears. She turns to me and now her voice is as the sea booming on the shore, strong and unrelenting,

'You need to hear Astarot's tale, it needs to be told. And you young woman, shame on you, you act without cause or reason, you act from ignorance, you act from fear and guilt and that is no place to come from.'

'That's the terrible thing, lassie' Astarot booms. 'Last night your own fear was your downfall.'

'My, *our* desire was for a Dragon, one of the green Caledonian dragons, a dragon who would help us! That green Sky Dragon tried to kill us and you…' I snarl at the tiny repulsive creature, 'helped it.'

'That Sky Dragon as you call it was not real, it was merely the light, the shifting shape that is the Northern Lights. And did not my Rak bring you here?'

He indicates the sharp featured raptor dragon that barely reaches his knee.

'That was the creature that attacked us!'

Astarot roars with laughter, 'This little raptor runt!'

Before anyone has time to react Tracy disappears and there is a flash around Astarot's head and now all that comes from him are muffled sounds through his jaw that is clamped shut in bonds of green light.

Tracy reappears beside Rak and draws herself up to her full height, which is about the same height as the raptor dragon and taps Astarot on the knee.

'And so you shall remain my Dragon friend until you learn some respect for this young *drakiwarreor* of yours. I think it is now more apt for Rak to tell the story.'

The tiny creature draws itself up to its full height - just above Astarot's knee and looks up the vast mountain that is Astarot.

Until now I had seen him as sharp featured with pointed teeth, pointed claws and wings that were as angular as the rest of him. The amazement on his face turns to laughter and as he laughs his face becomes rounder, transforming him into a pleasant almost jolly dragon. I'm astonished!

'Well *drakiathair* it is the first time I have heard you speechless.'

'Drakiathair – dragon father?'

Tracy nods, yes Rak is Astarot's son.'

'Much though it pains my father to admit it,' Rak says, though there is no bitterness in his voice, he says it in a very matter-of-fact way. 'I am the firstborn of the beautiful Gloriana and Astarot Emperor of Alba and the Ice Lands. Unfortunately, I didn't take after my beautiful *drakimathair* for looks though I did apparently take after a not often honoured line on my *drakiathair* side for my size and raptor-like appearance. My *drakiathair* attributed this to a curse he believed he had incurred for his poor treatment of my *drakimathair*. Fortunately, I took after my *drakimathair* in nature.'

He smiles such a sweet smile I cannot believe that I could ever have been terrified of him.

'When I came out to meet you it was as if the Aurora was guiding me. The Aurora led me to you. I am so distraught that your wing tore as I tried to help you.'

Regnatha turns to him. 'There is no need to apologise – you saved my life! And this,' she indicates her broken wing '…was worth it to unite me with a family I didn't know I had,

drakibràthair-màthair ' she pronounces the unfamiliar language hesitatingly, savouring the words on her tongue – *drakibràthair-màthair* dragon mother's brother – then flushes with pleasure as her uncle nods and colours with delight.

'That is a title that I never dreamt I would have and I am happier to be called that than any other.' Rak tells her. 'I am thrilled to find that I am your *drakibràthair-màthair.* It pains me that I was not able to save my beautiful *drakinighean-peathar* from injury.'

A tear rolls down Astarot's grey crumbled face, and Tracy relents and unclenches his jaw.

'Aye, son you of all your brothers do take after your mother, she was as sweet and gentle in nature as you have shown you are. For that I am truly glad.'

'My old mother before she ascended starward told me what would happen if I continued to behave as I was doing. Yet still I did not heed. I never really believed that my beautiful Gloriana would leave me and her beloved Alba never mind take our dear daughter to Set with Dougie Mackenzie in the hope it would not only improve her health but bring me to my senses.'

Rak looks in amazement at Astarot, he has never spoken like this before. Astarot goes over and carefully puts his wing around Rak and, to Rak's amazement, for the first time ever, embraces his son.

'Aye I never dreamt she would stay there. Though I had thought she would have returned for all our sakes.' Then the unsuspecting Astarot turns to me and says, 'I hope they are well?'

Regnatha and I exchange a look of concern.

'Gloriana?'

Reluctantly I shake my head.

'Agraciana?'

Regnatha looks up, 'Agraciana?'

'Your mother…'

Tears well up in her eyes, 'My mother, Agraciana.'

The silence slowly turns to being even more awkward. I know it is up to me to break it.

'We have not come with good news. For in Set it is not only the Dragon Keepers who have been slain... but all the Dragons,' I say haltingly. 'The reason for our quest is for help the Dragon Wars.'

He shakes his head 'I should have known. I suppose I did know, I just wanted to believe, when I saw your beauty...' Astarot turns his gaze on Regnatha.

I cannot bear the silence, so I continue.

'My mother was the last of the Dragon Keepers, or so I thought. I saw her slain and my Granpa Jonas hid me and a dragon egg. When I hatched the egg... '

He looks at Regnatha and she shakes her head.

Into the silence the sound of Tracy's voice, soothing as water, flows 'I think this is a night for storytelling. Sit down child and you, Astarot make yourselves comfortable for I think it will be a long night.'

So we sit telling our tales. I tell him the tale of the Death of the Dragon Keepers and both Astarot and Rak listen intently.

Speaking of it all the enormity of what has been kept hidden and secret from me suddenly hits me.

As I say the words, 'When they told me I was a Dragon Keeper, like my mother and father – they said if anyone found out the Dragon Slayers would kill me too.'

I am trembling from head to foot – telling it has brought it all back.

Tracy puts a gentle hand on my knee, 'There is no need to be afraid of what is past – and there is no need to blame yourself.'

As she says these words I feel a relief, I was not responsible for what happened and it is long gone. The thought soothes me, my whole body relaxes and the trembling dies away.

Then as I tell I how the Dragon Keepers were killed I see the story in a different way. The look in my mother's eyes as she died wasn't one of fear, I could see her love for me. That fills me with love and I find myself speaking of her love and courage. How she loved the Dragons so much – more than her own life, the only thing she loved more than the Dragons I realise, was me. I'm filled with love at the memory of my mother and as I bring my tale to an end I'm filled with great love for this, my new family.

I hadn't thought it possible to feel more love than I felt when I bonded with Regnatha as she hatched, but now I feel part of this Dragon family, and I know now what my father and mother felt – this great love for the dragons.

Astarot turns his ancient head towards me and asks, 'So what is it that you want of me?'

'We need the old dragons to come and help us. We have hatched new dragons, but they need training, they fought bravely against Vlast but they are too vulnerable to stand against his army. Their intuition has got us this far but now…I've come to ask for your help. For the old dragons to help us…' my voice tails away, echoing in the empty cavern.

Astarot shakes his head, 'Then you have wasted your trip. He spreads his wings in the vast empty space. 'This ancient wreck is the only old dragon left in Scotland.'

There is a flash of green across his face and a sounding of bells as Tracy lands to stand alongside him.

'You listen to that tale and that is all that you can say?'

She pulls herself up to her full height, this minute creature alongside the vast form of this ancient dragon – and it is her who seems to hold the power.

'This is an opportunity for you, Astarot – you are needed, your time has come. And the time for you to acknowledge your sons.'

'You more than anyone know that I cannot leave here, I am bound here for all time!' Astarot groans.

He lifts his hind leg and the rusting clank of shackles dragging across the ground rings out – but I cannot see them.

'These chains bind me to Scotland for all time!'

'What chains?' I ask.

Astarot shakes his leg and the rattling sound is heard again but by now all four of us are gazing intently at his leg.

'They aren't there!' Rak exclaims.

Astarot raises his leg and once more we hear the sound.

'Can you see them?' I ask of him.

He shakes his head, 'My eyes aren't what they were.'

'This is an opportunity to end the spell that binds you!' cries Tracy. 'The magic is weak, even the sound of the chains isn't so strong.'

Astarot roars in frustration, 'How can I? It's not possible! I am bound *forever!*'

Tracy shakes her head, 'The prophesy said that you are bound for all *time* – until the day when time stands still and the future stands before you.'

This seems to get through to Astarot. He stops tugging at the invisible chains and listens intently.

'Did you not listen to her tale? *She is the future*. They slaughtered the dragons and thought they had destroyed them all – but the eggs were hidden, time stood still as those eggs waited. Here, standing before you, is the *drakiabarnabarn* you never dreamt you would see. The only chains you have now are in your mind.'

He scratches his claw on the ground lost in thought then looks up at the sunlight streaming in through the cave.

'I will come with you child. I will help as much as I can.'

At his words he shakes his wings and the dust spirals up catching the light. We follow his gaze then there is a sound, a sound of rustling, like an ancient wood coming to life and slowly, majestically Astarot soars up towards the light. As he does there is the faint sound of chains clattering and falling, dissolving away as he soars up into the sky.

When he returns he dives into the pool and emerges refreshed, shaking himself spattering us with rainbow coloured drops and we laugh in delight at this new side of Astarot, more like a playful dragon pup than the old curmudgeon we first encountered.

'My son, my *drakimhac...*' the pause as Astarot says this is filled with love, it brings tears to my eyes it is so beautiful to feel.

'My beloved *drakimhac* will you be the Guardian of Alba while I am gone? I may be the last of the old dragons, but you, like young Azra and Regnatha, you too are the future.'

As Astarot asks this as a favour we see Rak grow before our very eyes. The stunted raptor is no more as he unfurls his wings and sweeps the floor in a great flowing gesture of Dragon obeisance.

Astarot lifts him up, 'No, my son, it is I who owe you respect. You have taught me, thanks to the goodness of your heart. I would gladly entrust our beloved Regnatha to your charge, for she is unable to return to Set, her wing, even healed, will not enable her to fly.'

'I would do that gladly...'

'But I ask a favour, a boon of my beautiful *drakiabarnabarn*. There is a dragon, a fine young dragon from Iceland. He would be a good match for you, my child, if you were to marry…'

'Marry!'

Again as one we exclaim.

The shocked cry is reverberating around the cavern. Regnatha pulls back in horror – and I stand in front of her, though what good I hope to do I have no idea.

'It is too much, I see.'

He bows low onto the cave floor in a sweeping gesture his tears flowing. Tracy collects them in a phial. I look at her in amazement. She just smiles, 'A dragon's tears of remorse and compassion are extremely rare.'

Seeing his tears Regnatha steps forward and touches him with her good wing. 'I know, *drakiafi* that you have my best interests at heart. It just feels a step too soon.'

'I feel that now, Regnatha my dear. I appreciate my suggestion comes from a fear that I may not see you again. I would love to do anything in my power for your happiness. All I ask is that you meet this *drakiflath*.'

Regnatha gives a breathkiss an *anallpòg*. I feel myself gasp as I watch her – this is the first time I have seen this special breathkiss of affection, a fiery kiss direct from the heart of a dragon.

'*Drakiafi* it would be an honour to meet this *drakiflath* – when you return.'

The Crystal Forest

I feel the urgency to return to Set – and Regnatha's concern for me. I am happier now that Rak is taking care of her, but now it is time to return.

'Come' Astarot bids me. 'I will show you a view of this beautiful land to take back with you.' So saying he holds out his wing for me to climb up.

Riding on the back of Astarot feels so different to riding on Regnatha. How do I compare it? It's the difference between being used to riding a horse then climbing onto the back of an elephant. The familiarity of flying with Regnatha hasn't prepared me for this at all!

He is a different dragon to the one we met on that first day in Alba. Now he is alive, even his scales seem a steelier, shinier grey more metallic. He circles in the sunlight above the cave and I revel in the sun, it seems so long since I have been in the open air! We soar into the air - he revelling in the freedom from his chains, me revelling in the sharp freshness of the Scottish air. The blooming heather gives a faint red-purple tinge to the landscape. I can see how close we are to the sea and now I see the mound.

'Arthur's Seat was the site of the old Camelot. In human tales there is great debate about where this Camelot really was. In truth it wasn't a place, it was wherever King Arthur and his Knights held their court. So it was here when they came to fight battles for the Castle of Women.'

I start to ask a question but Astarot stops me... 'These are stories for another time. Today we celebrate the beauty of this place. I want you to return to Set with better memories of this land than your arrival.'

So I settle into the flight and feel the wind in my hair and Astarot names the sights, sounds and smells that greet me: the scent of the heather in my nostrils, the May blossom forming white and pink hedgerows below us as we skim the treetops and soar over the castle and the city and the sound, the strange keening sound of the bagpipes.

'The bagpipes,' I exclaim, even more excited.

Astarot turns, curious to gaze at me, 'Why the interest, lassie?'

'Granpa taught me the bagpipes, without the bagpipes. Well, the breathing.'

The ancient dragon looks at me steadily.

'For the Dragon's Breath, so I could hatch Regnatha – and Cinaed.'

'Who is Cinaed?'

'The first Dragon I hatched.'

'You are bonded to another Dragon?'

'No I only hatched the egg he bonded with Prince Samardashee.'

Astarot nods, 'We have plenty tales to tell tonight.'

I watch the tiny people below us.

'Are you not afraid of being seen?' I ask.

'Not at all. These people do not believe in dragons. All they will see is a grey cloud floating past in the sky. They once lived in such fear of me that the myth of the Sleeping Dragon was created. But look below.'

I see people scurrying about their business most of whom don't look up at all and those that do look our way merely put up an umbrella or scurry into a shop.

We fly back over the castle and hidden by Arthur's Seat and into the pond that conceals the entrance to the cave.

As we dive into the water I hear another sound, a deep, deep rumbling.

'What is that?' I ask him.

'The volcano is waking.'

'What does that mean?'

'I'm the guardian of the volcano and we are bound, when my power failed it too lost its power, and has been dormant a long while, for *mega-annia.*'

This means that its fire is reigniting, its heat building up – and we must go while it is still cool enough for you to fly through.'

'Fly through the volcano!'

The others are breakfasting by the water under the dawn dappled clouds, I've sated my appetite on berries and nuts.

'Yes!' Astarot's affirmative rebounds echoing throughout the cave. The others look up as he continues. 'We need to travel fast and the volcano can help us bypass time.'

I look perplexed at Tracy who nods. Still I hesitate, I need some reassurance. There are so many unanswered questions. What if in taking Astarot and his raptor sons - the three who I still haven't met - to Set this upsets the balance even more as *The Handbook* says?

As if reading my mind, *The Handbook* opens. There is one word on the page:

'Trust!'

I smile wryly to myself and gather up my things into my backpack before I turn to Regnatha. Words are too much. I hug her. All I want to do is just hold her. Nestling my cheek on her neck, the comforting feel of her scales, so strong, so firm, that have supported me on this great journey. I feel a warmth on my head that spreads throughout my body and warms and comforts me. I know without looking what it is, a breathkiss an *anallpòg* . This I will take with me, it is, perhaps, all I need.

Rak whistles - at least that is the only way I can think to describe it. He blows through his nostrils while stroking his wing across his nose, creating a strange deep vibrating sound.

'Wrap your cloak tight,' Astarot tells me and we fly way down through the tunnels into the heart of the volcano. The surprise, for me, is that I think I know this underworld from my experiences in Set, but that was no preparation for this journey, and Astarot tells me as much.

'You haven't lived long, child. What you have seen is nothing, the tip of the volcano.'

At first the darkness is pierced by thin shafts of light that barely reveal the vast dark rock of the cavern wall.

Then there is a change in our surroundings. The rumbling sound has been getting louder and stronger and the heat is more intense.

'Cover up, Azra' Astarot directs me. He has no need to tell me twice, I pull Samardashee's cloak over me, shielding my face from the heat.

The cloak is so woven that the hood is transparent, so it protects my face while allowing me full visibility – and hearing. For now there is another sound, a sound so beautiful yet alien to me – the sound of singing, but no human voice.

'What is that?' I ask Astarot.

'That is the sound of the Crystal Forest.'

Soon we are in the midst of a forest unlike anything upon the earth. It reminds me of the crystals that Granpa and I used to grow at home, putting salt into water and marvelling at the fantastic shapes forming in the bowl. But *these* crystals are miles high! We fly between them, crystal trees so tall disappearing down, way down into the very depths of the volcano so far that we cannot see their roots. And there is light, but where from I cannot tell. Astarot calls out singing a song that harmonises with the Song of the Forest. It creates a current of air around us as does the rhythmic beat of his wings. That I am so grateful for, for now the heat is so great that even the cloak is barely shielding me from it.

'How are thou, Azra?'

'Okay.'

'Good – we need to go into the core and out again, so you need to focus on maintaining your own body temperature.'

This explains why he questioned me so closely when I was telling him of Set. All the time he was asking what skills, tricks that I thought were for just for fun, for my amusement. I thought Granpa Jonas was just playing games with me.

One trick I had forgotten that I knew – until Astarot drew it out from me. Granpa taught me this at first for keeping cool in the hot summer months on my rooftop room. He learnt this skill from a wise monk who stayed at court – and showed Granpa this ancient art that few can master, but he recognised in Granpa an adept with fire and taught him this to help him in his art and in the desert. The monk was taught to use it by learning how to melt snow, sitting naked in it. He, however, taught Granpa the reverse, how to sit naked under the scorching midday sun. Granpa Jonas in turn taught this to me. I thought it cruel at the time, making me sit under the midday sun, but now I appreciate what he taught me. For now I am able to keep my cool as we pass through the heat of the earth's core.

The cloak and Astarot's wings help me as I take time to adjust and can re-master the temperature balancing as we dive down through the singing crystals: we travel for miles to within sight of the earth's core. A sight I can only feel through closed eyes, if that makes any sense. It is so intense that I keep my eyes tightly shut yet still see the glowing red light through my closed lids. Then it's gone as we turn at a sharp angle and we are heading out the other side of the forest – until it is just a memory. The singing and the crystal light fade as Astarot zooms up through the earth's belly. The air cools, my breathing eases as does the pressure of the intense heat on my lungs. We are now back in more familiar territory – the coolness of the caves and the darkness.

I close my eyes and rest my cheek on my backpack. I feel secure in the harness on Astarot's back and I all asleep for I don't know how long. Then I hear a voice.

Meanwhile back in Set...

Astarot and I hover in a passage within the volcano.

'Are we there?' I ask.

'Yes – you may get down,' he tells me.

'You seem puzzled, Azra.' Astarot observes as I climb down from his vast back, using his great scales as footholds. He holds out his wing for me to step out onto to avoid the difficult manouevre onto his leg, and I slide to the ground. I'm dizzy and it takes a moment to regain my balance.

'You said we were by-passing time. What exactly do you mean?'

'Ah, you humans and time. Time isn't a piece of string. Time isn't real – it's a measure that you human beings have tried to impose, it's an illusion.'

'How can it not be real?' I demand. 'It took Regnatha and I months to fly to you – and then weeks for her to recover?'

'We have just flown to the centre of the earth and back out again. We have passed through the Crystal Forest; time is not the same when you do that. We seem to have come out shortly after you left, but it isn't always a clear-cut thing. Just don't be surprised if things are not quite what you expect, things might be the same – or not.' Astarot tells me.

'How do you know...'

I'm interrupted by a voice, a woman's voice, calling out. Quicker than a dragon's breath Astarot scoops me up with his wing and returns me to his back. He moves cautiously towards the sound and it's as if we are looking through a shimmering bubble at the scene before us.

Then I begin to see, if not exactly understand, what Astarot meant about bypassing time – for as I watch the scene unfold before me I realise that we have stepped back in time. The voice belongs to my Aunt Constance.

She lies bound hand and foot in the passage where she had created a diversion to warn me of King Samardashee and his men approaching. If ever I had doubted her that has disappeared, for she has risked her life to warn me of the danger.

There is the sound of a grown man weeping. Aunt Constance calls to him, but in vain, he is absorbed in his grief. She hauls herself like a caterpillar through the darkness towards him. Silhouetted in a slit of light at the end of the passage I can make out the bulk of a giant of a man crouched sobbing over a lifeless form in regal attire that must be the man I only know frombooks and by reputation – Vlast.

'Master. Master.' The giant sobs.

Aunt Constance sees at once that the situation is desperate.

'Hector! Cut me free!' she commands the sobbing man, turning her back and her tied wrists towards him. 'Free me if you want me to save him.'

Her voice reaches past his despair, releasing him from his helplessness into action. He doesn't know what to do for his master, perhaps this woman, who somehow knows his name, might. With her hands free Constance takes a bottle from her pocket and tips the entire contents into Vlast's unconscious mouth. Next, she tears a strip from her robe and puts it between his teeth. She binds his arm tight above where it is blistered and burned right down to the bone.

Behind our bubble wall we watch.

'Dragonfire,' says Astarot. 'The only thing that destroys in that way.'

When Constance reaches for the sword from Hector's hand at first he refuses, until she asks, 'Do you want me to save your Master or not?'

I'm still not clear what has happened, but I scream, 'NO! Don't do it!' at my unhearing Aunt.

The giant hesitates.

'Hector, the shock and magic of the Dragonfire will kill him if it reaches his heart,' she tells him. A glance shows that she is right, the fire has burned his arm below the elbow, but the dark red trace that marks the progress of the magic has already worked its way up to his shoulder. He gazes at her and a look of recognition passes over his face.

'Yes, you know me and you know that only I can do this.'

With both hands she raises the mighty sword and brings it down, slicing cleanly between the ball and socket of his arm. The dark purple-red-green stream of magic seeps onto the floor and over the ledge into the abyss. Meanwhile Constance has threaded a silver needle brought from the depths of her skirts and threaded it with spider's web, stemming the flow of his life's blood from the open cut and neatly closing the gaping wound. She removes the cloth from his mouth and slowly he comes around. For one brief moment he has no recollection of what has happened to him, and in that moment he looks at Constance's loving gaze and returns it. Then he sees where he is and memory returns. He glances down at where his arm should be.

'No!'

She watches as he remembers.

He sees the severed limb next to his body. 'You did this?' he asks Constance.

She nods. 'It was the only way to save you,' she tells him.

Now his face has assumed its old look – a guarded mask for his emotions and she has no idea if he will praise or condemn her.

It takes all his strength to stand. Constance reaches out to help him, he refuses.

'Take me to the Palace,' he commands Hector. Obediently Hector kneels to allow Vlast onto his back.

Hector steps out into the chasm and my heart skips a beat – has the shock unhinged him? Then I see Hector throws sand ahead of him, revealing an invisible bridge to the other side. Constance holds back she checks the pulse of the warrior whose lifeless body lies on the ledge. 'Ochamore,' is the only word that escapes her lips. Vlast calls out impatiently to her, 'Come.'

Swiftly Constance wraps the warrior's cloak around him, covering him completely and weighting it down with stones before stepping out onto the invisible bridge.

'What now?' I ask Astarot. 'What good is it coming here if they cannot see or hear us?'

'It will not last. We have travelled so fast, bypassing time, it takes a while to adjust and for us to become visible in this time-space realm.'

So we follow them.

We hear Vlast outlining his orders to Hector as they return to the Court.

The court is in pandemonium. The courtiers are dashing hither and thither.

Standing on the dias is Gertrude who, the moment she sets eyes on Vlast, takes charge. She beckons the court herald who sounds the royal fanfare and directs the hesitant Hector onto the dias and place Vlast onto the royal throne.

'Silence!' Gertrude commands. Silence descends as the Court take in the sight of the bloodied wounded Vlast.

'Beloved people of Set.' Vlast tells them 'Our wretched boy-King Samardashee is cursed and fulfilling his destiny. It was foretold that he would do this. I have fought the Dragon that he has made allies with - and am here to tell the tale!' He gives a moment for all to observe his battle wound.

'This woman,' he gives a regal inclination of his head towards Constance. Constance freezes on the spot, what will Vlast do to her? The courtiers move and murmur.

'*Lady* Constance Mackenzie, foretold it and for her perception and honesty was exiled.' Announces Vlast. There is a murmur, '*Lady* Constance' the emphasis is clear, Vlast has reinstated her title.

'Thanks to her we were forewarned, and thanks to her I am alive – bearing the ravages of battle with yet another Dragon, to save you from that cursed, mad Dragon-loving Prince who slaughtered my beloved brother, his own father.'

I can feel the tide of anger and approval turning in Vlast's skilful, manipulative hands. I feel a mixture of terror and admiration as I witness his powers of manipulation – and so too does Constance, she looks far more uncertain than when she was in exile and shunned by all.

At this point a commotion ensues, a strange woman, chalk-white of face with hair thick white curls and eyes so pale a blue they appear almost colourless, breaks through the throng.

Vlast halts the guards and beckons her forward.

She gives a curt nod of deference before launching into her rapid speech.

'Honourable Vlast I am a messenger from the White Folk…'

She gets no further for the court is abuzz, muttering. All I can make out is:

'White Folk are the stuff of legends.'

'White Folk? They don't exist.'

The woman glances around and is about to speak again when Vlast interrupts.

'Who are these White Folk? Surely they are just make-believe?'

Constance is sure he is play-acting from his tone of voice she is sure he already knows this.

The woman strikes her staff on the ground, ending the chatter and murmuring.

'I am Dybra, messenger from the White Folk who live in the underground city of Telus within the great volcano.'

A flicker of a smile passes Vlast's lips – so brief I almost doubt I saw it – as the court is shocked into attention.

'And what, Dybra, brings you to us?'

'A boy calling himself your King has come to us with a dragon.'

The name *Samardashee* is hissed around the room.

'Ah, that poor boy. He is somewhat demented since he killed his father.' Vlast tells her.

Dybra is stunned. 'He killed Qahir The Conqueror?'

Vlast nods.

Dybra falls silent.

'But honoured Vlast that is not all. For this dragon that this Samardashee boy-king has brought to our world has hatched out an army of dragons from within the very walls of our city. He has created a Dragon Army.'

Terror sweeps through the court as the words are repeated, '*Dragon! Army!*'

Vlast may look composed but his only hand clutches at the throne and his nails tear the velvet, and I am the only one to notice.

Gertrude seizes the opportunity.

'People of Set, I appeal to you, and to you Syed as our religious leader and moral guide – we must rid ourselves of this poor demented boy-King and appoint a worthy ruler in his stead to do battle with this dragon army.'

The Court as one agree.

Reluctantly the Syed steps forward.

'If that is the will of the people…'

The crowd roar, 'Yes. It is our will!'

The Syed steps towards the Great Cabinet behind the throne that houses all the sacred treasure of Set. He unlocks a drawer and searches. Eventually he brings forth an ancient scroll which he reads,

'By the power vested in me as Syed of Set. In the lamentable unfolding and revelation that our present ruler, King Samardashee, is no longer of sound mind and is acting against the best interests of the people and kingdom of Set. The people of Set have petitioned to overturn his right to the royal throne. I ask for confirmation in the time-honoured manner.'

And one by one the courtiers step forward, each firmly placing their hand across their right breast. All bar one step forward in this way. The last, the stable boy, steps forward with his arms firmly by his sides.

The Syed stops him.

'Do you know and understand what you are doing?' he asks the stable boy?'

'Aye. I do. I no more believe that King Samardashee is mad nor working against the interests of Set than that my own heart is false.'

The Syed nods, for he believes this youth is the only one in this court today who has spoken the truth. But the decision is clearly made and the rules are clearly set out. So King Samardashee is deposed.

But a kingdom without a ruler is not possible.

Vlast's henchman and guard move around the crowd chanting 'Vlast, Vlast, Vlast.'

'Who will you have as your king?' the Syed asks.

And the crowd call out as one, 'Vlast!'

Gertrude has positioned herself by the Syed's side. 'Crown him!'

'We must wait, we have no crown, Samardashee is wearing it.'

'Then use another!' Gertrude demands, sweeping her arm to indicate the collection of royal jewels and headgear.

At this the Syed's face lights up for the first time in this whole process.

He ignores the direction of Gertrude's pointing, at the bejewelled Imperial Crown worn by King Qahir on state occasions for any duties of the Empire. He walks past this to the insignia from ancient times. He picks up the simple headdress and to Gertrude's horror places it on Vlast's head.

'May the feathers of the eagle give you the vision and insight needed for a king. May these three feathers instill in you the faith, hope and charity of all great rulers of Set.'

But Gertrude will have none of this. She has gone to the Great Cabinet, which is still open, and removed the Imperial Crown. The rubies, emeralds and diamonds that encrust the gold crown make Gertrude stagger under the weight of it.

The court gasp as Gertrude, the first to dare to touch a sacred Imperial crown apart from the Syed or the King, holds it out to the Syed.

'This, oh revered Syed, is a more fitting crown for a King who has fought and given both his blood and body in the fight against the dragons. This is the Crown for him to lead his people into battle against the dragons.'

'Aye!' The response choruses throughout the Great Hall and the Syed has no option but to take the crown. Swiftly Gertrude takes the sacred feather headdress of faith, hope, charity and vision from Vlast and casts it carelessly to one side.

All eyes are now on the crowning of King Vlast and no-one but Astarot and I in our bubble world notice the feathered crown slip to the floor to be pushed under the throne with a swish of Gertrude's robes.

Vlast is elated, his chest thrusts out and he revels in the glory of the occasion.

'Our best warriors will rid us of this scourge. We will trap them in the very caves in which they have sought refuge, entomb them.'

The passionate speech exhausts him and the moment they withdraw from the throne room Vlast slumps against his Queen. The three women step forward to assist him. Gertrude removes the weighty crown.

Dybra checks his heart. 'He needs tincture of ruby.'

Gertrude turns to Constance 'You Lady Constance have the most powerful ruby in the land, surely you will give it to help your king?'

'Alas, it is no longer in my possession. King…' She stops herself. 'It was destroyed by Samardashee's warriors.'

Gertrude is so incensed at this she thrusts Constance's sleeve abruptly up her arm to check for herself. Sure enough Constance's hand lies unadorned, only the indentation remains which the ring had worn over the years.

Constance senses something changes then in Gertrude. For a moment the mask drops, the bare civility and politeness fall away and the hatred and jealousy she feels towards Constance are unveiled. Constance feels fear course through her body – for she sees that for Gertrude the ruby was the thing that made Constance useful to her.

'How unfortunate,' is all Gertrude says, and her meaning is clear that this is more than unfortunate for Constance.

Dybra delves into her pocket and produces an elixir.

'I have elixir of ruby,' she says.

Gertrude takes it from her and examines it closely before allowing her to administer any to the new king. Absentmindedly Gertrude caresses the crown on Vlast's head, smiling as she sees him regain strength. She whispers in his ear, words that no-one but he can hear. Vlast nods. Gertrude smiles and turns to the guards.

'Show Lady Constance and our guest to their rooms.'

Constance and Dybra are escorted away from the royal chambers.

Who to follow? We decide to see where Constance and Dybra are being taken.

Until now these women have had no connection, but as they walk Dybra and Constance exchange knowing glances as they are led deeper and deeper under the Palace. Even I know this cannot be to guest rooms.

The two guards become careless as the women converse together, seeming compliant – and that is when Constance seizes her chance. I see her hand in her skirts and she brings out a phial from her deep pocket. She pulls her shawl up over her mouth and nose and motions Dybra to do the same. They turn a corner and Constance flips the lid from the phial releasing its noxious fumes that with a single turn she wafts into the nostrils of the accompanying guards. Both men are caught unawares, stagger and collapse gagging. Constance steps over the guard to run back the way they have come but Dybra seizes her arm.

'This way, I know a way.'

And Constance has to trust her. She follows deeper, down past the dungeons to a wall that Dybra knows how to open – and suddenly there they are, in the cavern.

'Won't Vlast's men come this way?' Constance asks.

Dybra shakes her head. 'They will go on the rail wagon line. This is quicker, more direct – and known only to a few. Even Vlast does not know this entrance.'

So how does Dybra know of this? I ask myself.

They emerge at the bottom of a vast chasm. Constance glances up and sees the motes of dust forming a path in a shaft of light. Debraa's eyes follow Constance's gaze.

'Yes, that is the Invisible Bridge.' Dybra tells her.

Constance recognises, high above them, the path that she trod, so trustingly with Vlast and his henchman to safe his life, little dreaming that a few hours later she would be fleeing from him.

'So from here we can see the light but from up there the darkness looks impenetrable,' she remarks to Dybra.

Dybra smiles, 'That is what has kept us White Folk safe from you Settlers all these years. That and Vlast's protection.' She says this last sentence with a bitter laugh, for she too went to the Palace with a very different opinion of Vlast.

127

'I believed Vlast would protect my people because he valued their work and needed them to mine the gemstones. I was a fool not to realise that as soon as he has the throne that he would not need us anymore.' She shakes her head, 'Why were you so devoted to Vlast?'

Constance looks surprised. 'Devoted? I suppose I was, without thinking of it as that. I thought of him as my friend, the only one who kept in touch or came to see me.'

'But you were the keeper of the ruby.'

'Meaning what exactly?' Constance asks.

'Vlast coveted that stone more than any other. Did you not see his face when you told Gertrude that it was destroyed?'

'Then why did he not just kill me and take the stone?'

'A ruby given with love has so much power, immeasurably more than one that is stolen. If you had given him the ring, even with the love of friendship, he would have held such sway…' Dybra pauses deep in thought. 'That is probably why Gertrude is so jealous of you.'

'Gertrude jealous of *me*?' Constance cries out in disbelief.

She pauses and it's as if the past rearranges itself in her mind, and as she does both Astarot and I can see her thoughts. The pictures that appear as scenes from her life from a different perspective. She sees that Qahir did love her when he gave her the ruby. How the ruby has protected her all her life – she often wondered how she was never slain during the Dragon Wars when her sister and her husband were brutally murdered.

It all made sense now, why Vlast kept coming to see her. As she reviews her life she remembers the look that Vlast gave Gertrude when he found out that Constance no longer has the ring. Now I see that when Gertrude spoke in his ear, his nod of consent was giving her permission to do what she wanted with Constance.

Vlast's treatment of her had always tempered her view of him, so when others called him cunning, devious, brutal she would counter that she had not found him so, she had found him to be a true friend, caring of her. Now she saw that his care of her related to protecting the ruby, ensuring he always knew where it was, and that, one day, Constance would give it to him. She realised with a shock that if she had still had the ruby in that throne room she would have given it to him when asked for it. Given it without a second thought for herself and what protection it was giving her – or what he might do with it.

She tells her thoughts to Dybra in hurried breathless bursts as they make their way through the tunnels. At first she is not sure how much Dybra is taking in, it's as if Constance is telling herself these revelations – but Dybra stops and turns when Constance says this.

'What would Vlast do with it? With that ruby, given freely in love, he would be protected and his life force would increase. He might be able to procreate, for all these years he has desired a dynasty – and behind Gertrude's back has tried to sire children without success. This could make him potent, maybe even fertile. It could work to the good in him – but it could also increase his self-confidence, so he sees all that he does as right – no matter what. His destruction of the dragons started from greed, to access the wealth within their nests, now it is even more dangerous – it is motivated by fear.'

'So why did you and the White Folk help him?'

Dybra gives a sigh so deep it sounds like the regret of ages.

'Once the dragons were slain Vlast persuaded us he was our friend, that he would lead us one day into the light on the surface. He told us once he had built his palace of crystals he would keep us safe within the Crystal Palace, that it was a palace for the people of the volcano and that the Settlers would learn to accept us. Over time I too began to believe him.'

'So you worked for Vlast from fear of the Dragons?'

'Yes. Vlast told us he was keeping the Dragons at bay, preventing them from returning to their nests. We had worked for the Dragons from fear, that fear kept us working for Vlast. Only the Dragon Keepers weren't afraid of the power of the Dragons.'

Sounds vibrate through the tunnel walls – muffled, dull thuds. The women quicken their pace.

Dybra leads them through the secret underground passages that the wagons from Telus use to take the gems to build Vlast's Palace.

Then Constance cries out and trips. Dybra helps her up. A dark soft shape lies on the ground, it moves and a red glow comes from it.

'This is ruby light!' Dybra cries.

'Azi-Dhaka.' Constance exclaims as she recognises the body.

'He is one of the warriors who captured me.'

'So the ruby is in him?' Dybra asks.

'Yes, it struck them and disappeared.'

'Then we must cut it out and retrieve it.' Dybra tells her. Dybra cuts Azi- Dhaka – and as her crystal knife pierces his skin a drop of blood appears.

Constance stops her hand. 'He is alive!'

Dybra sits back on her haunches and looks at the still figure in front of her.

Constance feels his limbs and chest, watching his face all the while. 'His bones are intact. How can that be from such a fall?'

'They used to tell stories of warriors who sewed rubies into their bodies who did not die, the ruby's power protected them.' Dybra tells her.

'But I did not give the ruby to them in love, it shattered in a fight.'

'Sometimes the ruby chooses who will have it and for it to shatter and enter each and every one of those warriors sounds like a deliberate act.'

Azi-Dhaka listens to the women, taking in his situation.

'Oh Azi-Dhaka, so much has happened since you took me prisoner.'

She starts to tell him, but Dybra interrupts, 'We have no time for this.'

He looks askance at Dybra. She sees this and tells him, 'The ruby chose to conceal itself within you and the other warriors. That is enough of a sign for me. I trust the power of the crystals and the magic from the earth within them. They let me use their healing powers – and I see this as a message from the earth to trust you and the other warriors. Although I can see it may take you more time to trust me. Come, we must go for Samardashee has need of us.'

Now they hear more clearly shouts and explosions. In the darkness they see the ruby glowing in Azi-Dhaka's skin.

'Why is it glowing and itching like mad now?' Azi-Dhaka asks.

'It is warning of danger!' Dybra says, but too late.

Gertrude and her guards are upon them.

'You,' Gertrude points to one of the guards, 'Cut that ruby out of him.'

The guard hesitates, for his duty to obey his new Queen conflicts with harming the hero Azi-Dhaka.

'Your Majesty, this is Azi- Dhaka, Commander of the Palace Guard, the great Dragon Slayer.'

'I know who he is, and more importantly I am your Queen and have need of this ruby which he has concealed about his person.'

Azi-Dhaka looks into the young guard's eyes and the knife in the young soldier's hand clatters to the ground – he cannot kill this man, the man who has commanded him and the Palace guard his entire life, this legend.

The sound hasn't stopped echoing before the young guard falls beside his knife, his throat slit by the slender lethal blade that Gertrude carries in an innocent looking embroidered leather scabbard.

Triumphant Queen Gertrude she commands the remaining guards in turn and one by one the guards step forward, each trying to slit Azi- Dhaka's arm where Dybra had pressed her blade. Nothing. His skin remains intact.

Furious Gertrude steps forward, convinced that her men are being more loyal to Azi-Dhaka than to her she commands they hold him still. She wipes her blade clean on Azi-Dhaka's tunic then viciously cuts into him – or at least she tries. She can make no impression on his skin, he remains whole, the only thing that changes is that the ruby glows brighter, with a light that reveals its shape within Azi-Dhaka.

Dybra steps forward, 'The ruby is a talisman of protection and power.'

'But this one' Gertrude points at Constance, 'Is no longer under its protection.'

Dybra steps aside, exposing Constance to Gertrude's venomous gaze.

'That is true.' Dybra tells her.

And to their surprise this feeling of control and power over Constance's vulnerability lessens the tension.

Gertrude savours it. 'I always thought you were a bit simple, so stupid that you spent all those years bemoaning the fact that Qahir had tossed you aside for another.' She laughs and then she leads Constance out of earshot of the others.

'Confiding in my devoted husband that he was so *kind,* so *thoughtful,* so *caring* to risk coming to you in your exile. You never once guessed that he was the one who orchestrated everything. He was the one who slipped the potion into Qahir's cup that would make him forget ever loving you and make him fall for the first woman he set eyes upon.'

I watch Constance carefully, I'm sure Gertrude is telling the truth and that Constance believes her. At one time this would have turned Aunt Constance's world upside down. She has spent half her life believing that Qahir, the man she had believed to be her true love, had cast her aside. Now this woman, this woman who is jealous of her, who has just ordered her execution, is saying that it isn't the truth?

Lady Constance smiles, I see her own faith in herself and her judgement restored.

When Gertrude sees her words aren't having the desired effect, she tries again, twisting and turning her words even more. 'Vlast wanted your father and your family out of the way. With you as Queen and the Jonas family the most powerful family at court my beloved Vlast would have been outnumbered. A family of Dragon Keepers aligned to the throne was the last thing he wanted!

138

She picks a fern from the cave wall and takes it apart frond by frond as she speaks, 'One by one he rid himself of each of you so easily. How *easy* it was, and Silas Jonas, Lord of the Flame, the one he thought would be the most difficult he didn't even need to kill after all. It was more amusing for my Vlast to keep your pathetic old father alive.'

Her words were intended to destroy Constance's faith in her own judgement and intuition. But Vlast's betrayal gives Constance confidence – for it restores her faith in herself.

I now see things so clearly and a surge of happiness soars in me, I feel so happy for her I punch the air and cry out 'Yes!' The soldiers pause and look up, it's as if they can hear me.

But it's not me that they can hear. Gertrude has moved some distance away, sure that she is out of earshot – but the curve of the cave carries her treacherous words and the soldiers hear all.

One turns to Azi-Dhaka and lays his sword at his feet, the others follow in turn.

'I do not need your surrender,' Azi-Dhaka tells them.

'I have no wish to be a soldier and obey orders from one for whom I have no respect.'

Azi-Dhaka shakes his head.

'I no longer command the Palace Guard. I have no legiance to Vlast.' He pauses as it hits him. 'I have no allegiance to anyone or anything except my own honour and truth. If you want to come with me then you must follow your own honour and truth you are responsible for your own actions. I am no longer a soldier obeying orders, I am a warrior.'

This simple speech wreaks a change in all the men. When they lay down their arms they were soldiers, obedient trustworthy, disciplined – now as each picks up his sword they each give a different gesture, the first kisses his, the second raises his heavenward, the third holds his to his chest, the fourth breaks his across a rock and walks away. Yet all, including the one who walks away, are now grown as men, they are warriors.

As Azi-Dhaka and the three warriors move towards Gertrude her words falter. No exchange is needed for she sees at a glance that her command has gone. She turns and flees.

'Let her go,' Azi-Dhaka says. 'She rules through fear, there will be few of the Palace guard who will stand with her...'

As he says this suddenly there is another great explosion and it coincides with Astarot and I emerging into the swirling dust and falling rock of the Set time-space.

And all around me voices are crying out, *'Dragon!'*

How Fools Can Save the World

But back in the City things are at a very different pace.

At the time when Azra was setting off for Scotland she might not have left Set at all if she could have heard the determined Adib share his plans for hunting down her Granpa Jonas. But things are as they are –

and Adib had been given the nickname of 'The Wolf' for good reason and is hot on the scent of his prey.

When Constance was just freeing herself from her bonds and helping save the life of the man she still thought of as her friend, the two warriors Adib and Baligh were tracking down her father Silas Jonas.

Baligh does not try to stop him or hold him back, for Adib's blood is up. No-one hates dragons more than Adib, not even Vlast. Vlast's hatred is born of fear but Adib's is fuelled by his lust for revenge. A revenge that Baligh and the other warriors know only too well.

Adib returned from the Dragon Wars, from saving the kingdom and the Settlers from the scourge of the dragons, only to find that he had been unable to protect his own family. They had been savaged and burnt alive and their home razed to the ground.

Samardashee had chosen these two well to search the city.

Adib would hammer at the door with his staff, which would be answered for the sound was a familiar one to Settlers who had lived through these hard times. They knew what that knock heralded if they hesitated or delayed answering. Answering didn't guarantee safety but delay meant instant invasion of their home.

Once opened then Baligh, with his new-found eloquence from the ruby shard in his tongue, would enquire of the whereabouts of Silas Jonas. All Adib needed to do was weigh his club in his hand for the fearful Settler to answer immediately. And so they worked their way around the city.

Baligh's new-found gift of clear speech, after a lifetime of stuttering and self-imposed silence, gives him the confidence to ask for the first time how Adib, his brother-in-arms for many years, had come by his nickname.

For answer Adib bares his sharp teeth and says, 'The strength of the pack is the wolf, and the strength of the wolf is the pack.' Making even the stalwart Baligh almost flinch.

This was why Samardashee had picked his warriors – for they were while individually they were fearsome, together they were formidable.

They both know it is only a matter of time before they find Jonas. The answers of the Settlers bring them gradually closer to him, not by verbal information but from the subtle signs. Those who did not know of him were easy to tell apart from those who knew him but were too afraid to admit it. Adib watched the elders in the households, for they were the ones familiar with Silas Jonas, Lord of the Flame before he and his family fell into disgrace and his name no longer spoken. An old man's exclamation at Jonas's name eventually under Adib's persuasion gained them knowledge of the quarter he might once have lived in. An old grandmother's involuntary flicker of her eyes in a certain direction guided them, to the street. So they drew closer to their quarry.

Jonas meanwhile has returned home. Home to the house he hid Azra in for most of her young life, where he and his wife retreated into anonymity. He has decided he is too old to run any longer, in fact he is ready to surrender his life. The one thing that keeps him going is his desire to help his beloved granddaughter Azra. He's waiting – he is prepared to die but he is determined he will take whoever arrives at the door with him – less for young Azra to deal with. He prepares his traps and sits and waits, watching the door.

The hours tick by on the old clock and Jonas sits in the rocking chair – the one that Dougie Mackenzie found time and inclination to make all those generations ago in his years in Set. So Jonas sits, his hands stroking the arms of the rocker as generations of Mackenzies have done, both male and female. Sitting pregnant with

146

child or breastfeeding or whiling away time smoking – in the days when it was allowed. The peaceful motion is soothing in these times of fear and it calms Jonas. But his expectations are overturned when eventually there is a knock at the door.

The knock surprises him. Firstly in its tone – it's urgent yet not threatening. He stops the rocker and makes his way carefully towards it and unsnecks the door to see a sight he had never even dreamt of: two weary and disheveled figures that at first he doesn't recognise.

The dusty disheveled figure with a great belly, once Jonas looks more closely, he sees is wearing courtly clothes, as is his thin, bearded companion.

'Jonas, old friend, let us in.' Jonas recognises the voice of Lord Pacatore from the rotund courtier, and once he has that recognition he sees that the other is Lord Vruntled

'We are in grave danger.'
'We need sanctuary.'
The Lords beg him.

'Then you have come to the worst place. For I am expecting Samardashee's warriors to come for me. You could not have chosen a more dangerous place to come in the whole of the city.' Jonas tells them.

The two lords glance at each other. 'Then why stay here, old friend?'

'I am here to make it easier for them to find me – for whoever I can draw here is one less in pursuit of my beloved Azra.'

'Azra?'

'My grand-daughter.'

There is a look of great significance between the three men.

'So are the rumours true?'

'She is a Dragon Keeper?'

Jonas nods.

'Then we three are in the same boat. We too are being hunted, fleeing from the displeasure of the King.' The two courtiers laugh almost hysterically while the puzzled Jonas watches at first then joins in.

'Come. Let us celebrate! Make the most of this moment.'

So saying Jonas takes them in, guiding them carefully past his booby traps. He even finds some tobacco hidden in his illicit stash, homegrown amongst the plants in the tiny courtyard, and the last remaining bottle of fine brandy.

They smoke, almost choking on the unfamiliar pleasure of the tobacco, but enjoying it nevertheless.

Once they have broken one taboo and had a few drinks they are quite cavalier about breaking more.

Jonas does some of his old fire-breathing party tricks.

Pacatore joins in – he too was quite a fire-juggler in his day.

They have a night of reminiscing and jollity – of how when Jonas was Lord of the Flame they held magnificent acrobatic displays and fire juggling. Lord Vruntled, a gymnast in his youth, walks along the back of the old bench and around the room without touching the floor, balancing on window ledges and gripping his way with his fingers and toes along the carved door and window frames.

Seeing the weapons disguised as innocent household implements – the shovel and poker in the hearth, the sword hanging under a cloak, a spear disguised as a curtain pole, the lords delight in spotting Jonas's booby traps…and suggest more.

So when Adib knocks at the door they are prepared.

When the door remains unanswered Adib and Baligh burst in, but Jonas and his companions are men of great experience. The three fling open the door, so the hapless soldiers fall in as they put their shoulders to it.

Before they can recover they find themselves pinned to the wall with lethal knives thrown with deadly accuracy by Jonas, while Lord Pacatore scatters firecrackers round their feet, Lord Vruntled hurls rotten fruit that explodes in their faces.

The three are so excited that their deadly purpose dissipates and they continue though by now they are having fun, with Lord Vruntled nimbly prancing around the room with curtain cord to tie them, while Jonas blasts flame from his mouth – an act that disconcerts the two warriors who have not seen fire in almost twenty years. Lord Pacatore juggles poker, spear and frying pan with adept ease.

The time together has rejuvenated the old men, made them bold, and even Pacatore and Vruntled have recovered the bravery of their youth.

'So fine warriors, what brings you here?' Jonas asks.

'We come at the command of the King.' Baligh states.

'And what might King Qahir want with an old has-been like me?' Jonas asks.

'It is not King Qahir, may he rest in peace, it is King Samardashee long may he reign.'

This stops their japes.

'Is the prophecy fulfilled?' Jonas asks.

Baligh nods, 'The Palace is destroyed with fire.' They feel the mood of the room change.

Adib sees the sorrow in Jonas's face. The ruby shard pulses within Adib's heart. This warrior bent on revenge feels compassion for the old man, his one-time friend – who he knows could have slain him with any one of the knives that pin his garments to the wall. He knows this and to his own surprise feels gratitude that he is still alive. He tempers his words with more kindness than he has felt in many a year.

'Your daughter Constance is taken prisoner.' Adib tells him, not in triumph but as information.

Jonas knows that his daughter has powers that will keep her safe, so if this is the worst news that Adib has it gives him some relief which he can barely hide. His old friends can see what is going through his mind – for there is no mention of Azra nor of any dragon's egg either so they must still be free.

Then Lord Pacatore in his usual jovial way declares, 'We must sound the bells. Announce the death of King Qahir, may he rest in peace, and proclaim our new King – Samardashee!'

An hour before the three would have slit the throats of their captives, but now when Baligh asks, 'What of us?' their response is very different.

Seeing the two warriors pinned helplessly to the wall any fear the three may have had of them has turned to sympathy. They confer.

'I do not like to leave them here, even bound and gagged it would take no time for them to escape. I think we take them with us. They may prove of some use.' Jonas tells them. The two lords agree. Swiftly they unpin the two helpless warriors from the wall and hobble their feet and tie their hands.

As they set off through the deserted streets Baligh starts to laugh. 'What is it?' Lord Pacatore asks him.

Baligh shakes his head, 'Nothing, nothing at all.'

Then as they set off walking again, once more he begins to laugh. This time they insist he tells them.

'Now I see why you hobbled us. Now we walk like you do.'

They five set off walking again and it's true what Baligh says, the two warriors hobble along at the same pace as the three old men. The laughter spreads, and even stern-faced Adib smiles at the joke. So within a short space of time the five men become travelling companions.

They break into the City bell tower and sound the grandsire bell – the death knell, making public that the King is dead. Then they sound the carillon bell – to announce the new King. Still the streets are deserted.

They look at each other, 'Are the people so afraid they won't even come out for this?' Baligh asks.

'They must not know what it means,' Jonas tells them.

So when they come across a young boy asleep in a doorway Lord Vruntled presses a gold coin into his hand, 'Go, spread the news. Tell all that King Qahir is dead, long live King Samardashee!' As the boy begins knocking on doors and calling out the news, one by one heads start appearing at windows and Settlers start to throng the streets.

'We must make haste,' Jonas tells them, 'We need to reach our destination before nightfall.'

Adib asks, 'Where are we going?' `

Jonas ignores him and Baligh shakes his head at his companion as he is about to ask again, for he can see that Jonas will not reveal this.

Azra's Return

As we fall through the time bubble into Set, I hear the cries of 'Dragon' – but for the first time this isn't a cry of fear.

All around us rocks and dust and debris tumble but the cries from Constance and Dybra and even from the warriors are of amazement and welcome, the first time I have heard the sound of relief in the word 'Dragon'.

Astarot lands amid the rocky scree and uses his wings to maintain his balance while his claws search for a foothold. He is running across the shifting tumbling rocks and earth that is falling away beneath our very feet. His call is clear – they may not understand the language, but instinct means they know this is their way out. All cling to the only thing that isn't falling – even Azi-Dhaka the Dragon Slayer – for the fear that drove him before, fueled by his loyalty to the King – has now gone. His instincts have taken over and the ruby that saved his life, giving him invincibility, has also given him greater insight and affinity with the very dragons that he once slaughtered.

He reaches out instinctively and seizes onto one of Astarot's great claws. The others seize hold of Astarot's legs and massive tail and this great creature its giant wings beating a steady rhythm takes us up and away from the cascading rocks and dust, along the underground river, towards the underground city of Telus.

Vlast's men have dynamited the city itself. The mighty walls of the volcano vibrate with explosion after explosion pouring clouds of dust, rocks and gems onto the town. Samardashee astride Cinaed, the beautiful dragon he hatched, is clearly in charge.

'Cinaed – we have to fly these people out.' Samardashee tells him, feeling more and more the weight of the responsibility that all his training as a Prince have failed to prepare him for.

'And risk once again wiping out all the dragons?' the young dragon says. But as he looks around Cinaed knows that his bondfather is right.

'Who knows, Azra may have found more dragons if there is a world left beyond Set. One thing for sure, if we stay here none of us will survive,' Samardashee says.

'We dragons can retreat to the Earth Core,' Cinaed responds.

Cinaed knows as well as Samardashee that this is not an option for the Settlers or the White Folk – the heat would destroy them.

Cinaed looks around at the destruction, then roars. His call halts all the dragons in their tracks and they are swiftly at Cinaed's side. Samardashee admires the young dragon's natural leadership.

The consult briefly in *Draco*, too fast and fluent for Samardashee to understand with his limited grasp of the language. He cannot tell whether it has gone for or against, but the dragons have agreed they will help fly them all out but there is an unexpected footnote to the rescue.

'We will take you all out,' Cinaed tells him. 'Then we will go into the Earth Core.'

The dragons are the one thing protecting the Settlers from Vlast and his men. The fear of the mythical beasts is their only real protection.

This, however, is no time for Samardashee to argue. All he can do is to face each challenge one step at a time. He doesn't want to waste time worrying or arguing about what might happen when the dragons leave. For now he is happy that the dragons will fly them all out.

As the humans climb onto the dragons to begin the evacuation another explosion causes a rock fall. Cinaed turns to

Samardashee with a baring of his teeth and an expression that the young King would call a wry smile — if it was on anyone's face but a dragon's.

'Well you have your wish, bondfather.'

'My wish?' asks Samardashee, puzzled.

'The entrance to the Earth Core is now blocked.' Cinaed nods towards the latest devastation. 'Now humans and dragons share the same fate.'

So the evacuation begins.

At first some of the White Folk are reluctant to climb upon the dragons' backs but another explosion galvanises them into action and the four young dragons fly swiftly through the vibrating corridors of the underground system taking the White Folk up out of the volcanic shaft to safety.

Samardashee and his men are the last to fly.

He shields his eyes as they emerge from underground into the sunlight and there,

standing in the sunlight, the White Folk stand entranced.

They have spent their lives in the half-light of the volcano – and now they are in the glorious technicolour of the sunlit world. They shade their eyes at the brilliance of it.

This glorious new world amazes and entrances them. Some hold their hands over their eyes peeping between their fingers at the bright blue sky. Others are laughing and weeping in wonderment. For some it is too much – they are temporarily blinded at the light.

Farshid, sunshine, someone whispers and the whisper passes around.

But those who have become accustomed to the light are amazed at the vastness of the desert and the sky.

Their perspective is not like Samardashee's, some reach out to touch the sky – for to them it seems as close as the cavern walls that they are used to below ground. One stumbles forward, puzzled, still reaching out.

162

It is amidst this confusion that Astarot lands with his diverse cargo. I slide down his wing to land beside Samardashee.

'They have no depth of vision, poor things,' I exclaim.

'Azra!' Samardashee cries out, 'I thought you had left?'

'I did. I've brought help.'

I gesture through the smoke and dust surrounding the vast grey mountain that is Astarot, so easily mistaken for part of the very fabric of the volcano, moves. Samardashee stares at the megatron in amazement.

Astarot whispers in my ear, or as near to it as he can get, 'I warned you.'

'What is this creature?' Samardashee asks as he draws his sword.

'I am not a what, I am Astarot, Dragon Emperor of Alba and the Ice Lands.'

'Where did you find him?'

'Scotland,' I reply, 'And you better not insult him.'

'Impossible!' Samardashee exclaims. 'You only left a few hours ago.'

I dart a glance at Astarot, daring him to speak, he shrugs his great scaly shoulders, releasing clouds of dry scaly dust and snorts.

'I have been gone months,' I tell Samardashee, 'travelling through the centre of the earth changes time or something.' I need to stop him asking more questions, 'What is important is that this is Astarot, Guardian Dragon of Alba.'

'This is a dragon?'

'Yes, and he must return at once to the borders of Set, which his sons are guarding for us, to avoid an imbalance, for disaster will surely strike if he remains.'

Samardashee laughs, 'Disaster! What is this?'

He gestures to the chaos around us.

'Er... well. That is what *The Dragon Keeper's Handbook* said,' I end lamely.

Constance overhears us.

'Sometimes *The Dragon Keeper's Handbook* can be out of date.' she tells me.

'Meaning?'

'What one Dragon Keeper wrote maybe hundreds or perhaps thousands of years ago may not be true today.'

Samardashee nods, 'I think your Aunt has a point.'

'Besides, when the Dragons were slaughtered there were none and that would surely cause an imbalance.'

'So how do I know what to trust in the book?' My heart sinks as I realise just how much I have relied on *The Handbook*. Since Reggie stopped arguing with it I've taken every word as literal truth. At this *The Handbook* nudges at my back. I take it out and it opens itself,

'Don't believe everything you read.'

I stare at it, stunned. 'So I'm not to believe you?'

'You need to question everything. For whatever you read or hear is merely someone's opinion. You need to make sure it stands up with what you know to be true for you.'

'But you are The Dragon Keeper's Handbook!'

'And what is writ in me is written by the Dragon Keepers - and they are only human.Look at how much you have changed your opinions and beliefs since we met.'

I close it carefully, having read it aloud.

Samardashee looks me straight in the eyes, 'Disaster is already upon us.'

My stomach flips. It's as if I am seeing him for the first time and I can see right into him. His words may sound hopeless, but he is not, and he is no boy. This is no longer the little Prince from the tales

Granpa used to tell me. He is no longer the innocent, or some may say ignorant, Cursed Prince. Whether or not he is King, for certain sure he is a warrior. Like the dragons the events of the past whatever they are - days, weeks, months the timescale is irrelevant. These experiences have changed and matured him.

'We need all the warriors together,' Constance says.

'The warriors are all with Vlast,' Samardashee reminds her, and reluctantly I let his gaze go.

'They are not warriors!" Constance exclaims. 'They are drones, mere puppets of Vlast, whose own strings are tweaked and knotted by Gertrude's cunning avarice.' She pauses for breath, taken aback by her own passion. 'The warriors we need are *the* warriors, picked by a power other than man – *The Warriors of the Ruby Shards.*'

As she says those words something in them stirs in the people, a feeling of hope, a feeling of strength.

167

'Who are they?' asks Azra.

'They are the Warriors that the ruby chose to hide within. In times of trouble when all are seeking with lust and greed a stone may choose to divide and it picks its hosts most carefully.'

Samardashee snorts in disbelief, 'The ruby you talk of shattered, destroyed. It did not *choose* to hide in us.'

As he says this the ruby within his eye stirs and brings him to his knees. Azi-Dhaka moves involuntarily, resisting as much as he can but he too ends up, kneeling alongside Samardashee before Lady Constance Mackenzie.

'I'm realising more about the power of the ruby as I see it in others than when it was in my hands,' as she looks tenderly on the struggling men. 'Be still. The ruby is the Heart's Blood of Mother Earth. When you are at ease with it, it can guide you; if you fight it you will only feel pain and suffering.'

The two men cease their struggle and the pain leaves their faces. Azi-Dhaka watches in amazement as his skin changes colour. His dark brown arms become golden and translucent as he allows the strength and power of the ruby to flow through him.

Samardashee looks around and now it's not through his human eyes that he is looking at the world and people around him, but through his ruby eye. The tension and determination leaves his face and he breathes more easily as he uses his ruby eye.

Both men now feel the strength and power that the ruby within gives them. As I watch Samardashee my heart reaches out to him for the responsibility on his shoulders. We are of an age and I would not want Samardashee's cares on me.

'It does not look too disastrous for them,' I tell him as I watch the White Folk.

These same Folk who had staggered from the twilight of the volcano, wailing and grieving their dead, are laughing and weeping in wonderment. Dybra is gathering them together.

'What is happening with them,' I ask Astarot.

He nods, recognising what is happening, 'People who have been living underground so long, can be transformed when they emerge into the sunlight and fresh air. With me it wasn't so dramatic - I had access to light and air, albeit for a limited area around the Seat.' The Seat, Arthur's Seat so many hundreds of miles away and the thought of my Beloved Regnatha aches as I wonder how she fares in the lands of the Scottish.

Some of the White Folk are almost drunk on the fresh air, staggering, rolling in ecstasy on the ground. Some are sitting breathing deeply. Others sit transfixed at the bright flowers in the desert landscape, while some are reveling at the vastness of the skies.

I watch as the things that I take for granted as everyday astonish and amaze the

White Folk. I see Samardashee observing this too.

Then, as the golden globe of the sun changes the sky, the White Folk all come together encouraged by Dybra to watch the wonder of sunset for the first time. She talks soothingly to them and an air of calm comes over us all as we watch this daily wonder that I have so often take for granted.

'Will the sun harm their pale skin?' I ask out loud.

Astarot clears the dust from his throat. 'The ancient tales talk of how the peoples of the Earth grew in the very ground and when they emerged like seeds they were so pale, so white that they were called The White Folk by their fellow creatures. But over the months their pallor changed. Those that spent most time out in the sun darkened and turned golden brown, those that kept to the dappled shade under the trees, their skin blushed the colour of peaches. The fisher folk and the desert folk turned different shades of yellow, brown

171

and some a shade of ebony so beautiful and glowing you could lose yourself in it. The shyest folks on earth their skin turned green or earth-coloured to camouflage them wherever they were on earth no matter the season, so stories grew up around whether they even existed at all. All the colours of the rainbow were found in those Earth seeds of the first White Folk from deep within the bowels of the Earth, while others remained as they had been, and that was good too. They will adapt as they see fit.'

'They seem to have no cares now,' I observe.

Samardashee is now calm himself.

'They have no need for panic, they are safe here, for the moment. That is all that matters to them.

'What of the future?' I ask.

Samardashee smiles – since he has stopped fighting it, the ruby has soothed him.

'We will think of that tomorrow.'

'But where are the other warriors?' I insist.

Samardashee pauses for a long while, reluctantly dredging his memory.

'I sent Baligh and Adib to the City to...' he hesitates, 'to find Silas Jonas.'

But his softening of words does not fool me, 'You sent them to hunt down my Granpa!'

It's not a question, for I know I am right. I am mad at myself for going to Scotland before I made sure Granpa was safe, mad for ever believing I could trust Samardashee the Cursed Prince.

For a fleeting moment I see what might have been a flicker of concern pass over Samardashee's face, but the blissful effect of the ruby takes over and he lies down. He pats the space beside him, 'Come, sit with me. Watch the sun set.'

But I will have none of it. Looking at him now I wonder how I ever let my heart open to him. 'I must find Granpa before they do.'

I stride to where Astarot is resting, eyes closed. The second I touch him his eyes open, alert, ready.

Samardashee calls out, 'They were not to kill him.'

But I am already mounted onto the Dragon's back. 'There are some things worse than death, and your Warriors are trained in those ways' I yell at him.

'How did I ever think he had grown up?' I ask myself.

Azi Dhaka races towards us and hangs onto Astarot's claw as we take off in a flurry of dust that makes Samardashee choke on his words.

'Do you want him with us?' Astarot asks me.

'A warrior on our side might be useful – if we can trust him!'

The Trackers Tracked

As we fly it's like I'm travelling back in time – as I see below me the Forest of Discontent and the trail we followed to Lady Constance's caravan, the aunt that until that day, I never knew existed. Back to the City of Set where I used to lie in my rooftop bed tracing the stories in the stars, yet not once did I picture myself flying back to my home on this ancient Dragon. The place seems strange, familiar yet not. I am hesitating at recognising the once familiar landmarks. When I tell Astarot he replies, 'That's because you have changed.'

I know he is right, I am not the shy, reclusive girl used to hiding in my nest bed on the roof.

'You're a warrior now,' Astarot says.

'I'm no warrior – I didn't fight the battles.'

Astarot shakes his great head, dust showering from his grey scales.

'A warrior is someone who protects the earth, who nurtures it and cares for it. When you are a true warrior there is a quality about you – a quality which you have. The people here do not have that.' He indicates the houses where the sleeping Settlers have yet to wake to the new day.

'They are asleep in more ways than one. They need to wake up and come out of hiding, as you did.'

We turn a corner and I stop, dumbstruck. The house, my house, stands burnt out, the roof, doors and windows gone as if blasted out by the great heat.

Astarot glances at the smouldering ruin, then at me. 'Is this it?' he asks.

All I can do is nod. I cannot speak, my throat is choked and I know I will start crying if I do. The emotion it brings up surprises me, I realise this was more than just a house it was a home for me. I did feel safe on my bed on the roof and now it is gone. Only the shell remains, as empty as an abandoned Dragon's shell once it has hatched.

The street is silent. Nothing stirs.

Azi-Dhaka strides to the house next door and knocks, hard – the door swings open. One glance shows that it too is abandoned. It's the same with the house on the other side.

Astarot, too big to enter by the doorway, has flown onto the roof and removed a precarious beam and reaches one great foreleg down into the ruin, his claws sifting through the rubble while Azi-Dhaka searches on the ground. A feeling of dread fills me, I mutter to myself, 'I know that everything always works out for me. All is well.' It comforts me and I gasp in relief, only then do I realise that I've been holding my breath. I gulp in the air then start to breathe more easily. Then I glance up at him and he shakes his head before flying down to land beside me.

'It's all right. There is no-one in there.'

Astarot looks at me. 'You have grown, Azra, you are in charge of your emotions. You do not let them overwhelm you.'

'I've become hardened,' I tell him.

He shakes his head. 'No. You have a kind and loving heart, you are not hard-hearted, you just don't let fear take a grip on you as you did in the past. You don't let fear take over.'

We scan the ground for clues. There are lots of footprints up close to the walls – the route the fleeing neighbours have taken, then I spot that there are only a few tracks that cross the street. Three sets of footprints close together – one with Granpa's distinctive limp.

'They must have taken him prisoner.'

'No,' says Azi-Dhaka, 'those two sets of soldier's boots are too close together, as if they are hobbled and they are walking in front; those other sets are soft-soled leather shoes. His friends' must have helped him escape. could they have taken the warriors prisoner?'

'Granpa? He has no friends, and how on earth could he take two warriors prisoner?' I exclaim.

'You know him as your grandfather, at Court The Lord of the Flame was legend. Things change. When he was hiding you to have friends was dangerous, anyone who knew of you was a potential risk. Now – he needs friends and maybe he has found some.'

The tracks merge in the confusion of footprints in the dust.

'So what now?' Azi-Dhaka asks.

I sit down, exhausted, and shrug. As I ease my backpack off and pull out my water bottle something falls out. I ignore it.

Azi-Dhaka picks it up and tries to flick through it, but it remains stubbornly closed in his hand.

'What is this?' he asks.

With a sigh I take it from him. 'It's *The Handbook*, *The Dragon Keeper's Handbook*.'

I stop, my curiosity piqued as it opens itself to a picture.

'You see something?' Azi-Dhaka asks.

'It's odd. It's a picture of what looks like Granpa – smoking and drinking with two men.'

'Describe them,' he demands, eagerly.

'It can't be Granpa – he doesn't smoke or drink,' I insist.

'*No-one* has smoked or drunk for sixteen years – officially,' Azi-Dhaka reminds me.

'Describe the two men,' he repeats.

'One is tall and thin with a pointy face and a beard, the other is short and fat...'

'...with a ruddy complexion.' Azi-Dhaka finishes, he smiles and strikes his knee. 'Well I'll be blowed... I'll bet my shirt that those are Lord Vruntled and Lord Pacatore, if I'm not mistaken. They were at court with your Granpa. I think this could be a reunion of old friends.'

I look at the illustration in amazement. 'Friends? Granpa has friends?' And a warm glow comes over me.

As we make our way through the City we see that already things are changing – smoke curls from fires that have never been lit in my lifetime. I sniff the air at the abundance of wonderful smells. Azi-Dhaka and Astarot help me identify them: the smell of baking bread and cooking meat; the strange burning hay, horse dung like smell of tobacco drifts across my nostrils as old men and old women bring out their clay pipes and hookahs.

On the outskirts of the town the blacksmith has cleared the rusting junk from his old forge and is working the bellows to fan the fire, for once again he can shoe the horses properly.

We pause to watch the wondrous flames as they lick and shoot up into the air as the bellows feeds them. The blacksmith turns and grins a sooty grin.

'Is that you, young Azra?' he asks me.

'How do you know me?' I demand, puzzled.

'You are the image of your mother. There are more than your Granpa can keep a secret in Set. I think it is time you had this.' He goes to the back of the forge and removes two bricks carefully and removes something wrapped in sacking. 'This was your father's,' he said pulling a slender sword from within the parcel. 'And this was your mother's pulling out a headband with an emerald set in the centre.'

He hesitates, looking first to Azi-Dhaka as if to ask if it is more appropriate for him to do the honour.

Azi-Dhaka shakes his head, 'The smith is more of a priest than a warrior. It is more fitting for you to do this.'

The blacksmith washes his hands carefully before polishing the headband gently with the silk cloth that wraps it before placing it upon my head. The emerald rests in the centre of my forehead and in the light of the fire its green rays sparkle around the smithy.

A hush comes over my travelling companions and the smith and Astarot kneels before me,

'All the green of nature is in the emerald, it stirs the soul like the heart of spring. She symbolizes hope, truth and the future and needs to be worn by a Seeker of Love and a Revealer of Truth. (Hildegard von Bingen)

183

Those are not my words; they are from a human with more insight even than I on this.'

I know instinctively that this is not something to protest at. We four are lit by the glow from the fire and the light from the emerald moves around the room each time I shift my gaze. At last I pull my hood over it.

The mood has changed, there is a calmness amongst us now.

'If you seek your Granpa he was headed in that direction.' The blacksmith shows me.

'The Forest of Discontent?' Azi-Dhaka asks.

He nods and turns his attention to the anvil.

'Was he alone?'

'It might be better he were alone,' the blacksmith said.

'For why?' asks Azi-Dhaka.

'For he was in the company of those two fools…'

'Vruntled and Pacatore.'

The smith nods, 'And most bizarre of all they had two warriors held prisoner. How long that ship of fools could continue is only a matter of time.'

The Jaws of the Dragon

We proceed cautiously once beyond the city. At any sign of life, be it human or animal, the Astarot curls himself into a ball like a great granite hillside. We adopt this strategy as the best available. It may astound any Settlers to see a great rock appear in the landscape, but as we too express astonishment at this landscape phenomena and add that these are changing times our explanation goes down far more readily than the sight of a dragon would.

We halt on the outskirts of the Forest of Discontent – unwilling to follow the trail in the dark.

As we settle for the night there is a sound in the bushes. Instantly Azi-Dhaka is on his feet sword in hand. But one glance and I see there is no sign of the ruby light in his skin. Astarot breathes a glowing arc of firelight to reveal...

'Granpa!'

I rush towards him and suddenly I'm an eight-year-old hugging this man who has been my rock throughout my life. I'm laughing and crying and staring up at his lovely, grizzled face aglow in dragon light.

Beside him are two men as old as he, whom he introduces as Lord Vruntled and Lord Pacatore.

Astarot and Granpa light a fire – though Azi-Dhaka protests at first about this, saying it will attract attention.

'There's no need to teach me to suck eggs, Azi-Dhaka. Have you forgotten who taught ye the secrets of fire when you were a lad?' Granpa Jonas tells him.

He lays a fire that gives a heat to warm us, yet the glow remains within our small circle.

'Yon two warriors are encamped at Rufus's place and he has fed and watered them well.'

The three old men chuckle amongst themselves.

'What do you mean, Granpa? You haven't hurt them?'

'No, my dear, I wouldn't do that. We just made sure that they will get a good night's sleep with a little potion. So we have no fear of being disturbed. Rufus is watching over them.'

I smile at the mention of Rufus. Rufus was the name of our old horse, reliable and dependable, safe. It was also the name of the tinker, who lived in the Forest of Discontent, and it wasn't just his name that reminded me of my old horse, he too had a quality of reliability and dependability about him. I felt safe knowing he was taking care of them.

We sit around the fire throughout the night, swopping tales of our adventures. The old men toasting each tale in whisky from a bottle Astarot produced tucked under one of his scales to the great delight of the three old timers.

Granpa Jonas looks at me with such pride and amazement that I blush as I tell of my time in Scotland. And my jaw drops when I see him give Astarot an affectionate slap on the rump as I tell of how the dragon has taken care of me and brought me safely back to Set.

'Aye you Caledonian dragons aren't so bad after all. As for you Azra, I told your Gramma that blood will out, no matter how much she tried to keep things from you. You're your mother's daughter, no doubt about that.'

When I insist that Granpa Jonas and Lord Vruntled and Lord Pacatore tell their tales we all end up holding their sides roaring with laughter, tears rolling down their faces. I don't need whisky to be as merry as they, nor to my amazement does Astarot who joins in the good humour in a way that is nothing short of miraculous.

Lord Vruntled imitates Lord Pacatore's hallucinations in the desert, seeing chicken mirages. Not to be outdone Lord Pacatore tiptoes around, using Astarot as stand-in for the horse they had, mimicking Lord Vruntled's high-pitched tones to a T. It is only when Astarot joins in, roaring with laughter and hiccoughing flames, that they call a halt. We fall asleep around the burning embers until dawn pinks the sky.

Granpa Jonas wakes me and we move into the heart of the forest to find Rufus the Tinker.

Throughout this Azi-Dhaka is more subdued. Once he hears his warrior companions are safe he seems more relaxed but when he learns they have been doped he is more cautious and like me does not drink.

Granpa is very wary of him – he is sure Azi-Dhaka is sizing him up, waiting for an opportunity to strike.

'Of course he will,' I tell him, 'for you are doing the very same thing to him. If you don't trust him, he won't trust you.'

Granpa is startled, 'Where did you pick this idea up?'

The Dragon Keeper's Handbook jumps into his lap and opens itself. He stares down into a blank page, disappointed that he cannot read anything.

So I read for him:

'Trust. It is important that you start from a place of trust, for if you do not have it in yourself then you will never be able to see it or believe it in others. You have to trust first then you will attract to you those who are trustworthy.'

Lord Vruntled and Pacatore nod in agreement. Granpa slaps his thigh and proclaims, 'Well, if I can trust you two fools and scoundrels then I am sure it's an easy step to trust this warrior.'

They hug and Azi-Dhaka tells him, 'How can I not trust the man who taught me so well as a child?'

As we arrive at Rufus's cabin in the clearing in the woods he appears at the door. The two warriors Adib and Baligh sit, blankets around their slumped shoulders.

Rufus holds Granpa Jonas back a moment, 'Be careful old friend, for this man is still sorely wounded at the destruction of his family. Let me tell him my tale first before you ought else is said.'

Granpa agrees. He wafts a smelling potion under their noses and instantly the two warriors are alert and on their feet. They greet Azi-Dhaka enthusiastically.

'I trust you slept well?' Rufus asks the two warriors.

'Too well for my liking,' Adib tells him, suspicious that Rufus may have doctored their evening meal. He refuses Rufus' offer of refreshment and guardedly makes his own meal. 'I recommend you do the same,' Adib tells Baligh. But Baligh merely breaks the bread that Rufus has brought him and gets Rufus to eat some before partaking of it himself.

'I gave you a potion to help.' Rufus tells them. Adib half rises, his hand on his sword but Rufus shows no fear.

'If I was going to do you harm wouldn't I have done it while you slept?' Rufus asks.

Adib concedes this.

'I heard you talk yester evening of your family.' He hurries on as he can see he has already touched a nerve in Adib. 'You talked of how you believe the dragons killed them.'

Adib is angry, 'The dragons slaughtered my family and burned our village to the ground.'

'Why do you say it was the dragons?' Rufus asks.

'I saw what they did, their brutal wounds on my wife and child. I'm just thankful we arrived when we did. At least we could bury them.'

'I too saw them, they were savagely ravaged,' Baligh affirms.

Without a word Rufus brings out a rusted, battered device, metal jaws burned black with use. He lays this at Adib's feet.

Adib looks up, questioningly.

'Vlast's henchman commissioned this from me. I was surprised when he wanted it repaired for fire was already banned. He wanted the jaws sharpened and to ensure the fire mechanism worked. He collected it the night your family were attacked.'

'Hector was a brute of a man.' Baligh says.

Adib examines it, looking as wolf-like and cautious as his name.

'This was used in the old days for the Fire Ceremonies,' a voice in the doorway tells him, revealing himself as a silhouette to the two. The two warriors are on their feet, swords at the ready in an instant.

'Fear not, we mean you no harm,' the figure says throwing his weapon into the room.

'And I think you know that – for I could have slit your throats back in the City.'

As the figure moves into the light he no longer looks like the stooped grizzled figure I used to know. This is not the shuffling, bent, old man of even a day ago, this man is The Lord of the Flame, Silas Jonas. He stands erect and moves confidently. He is accompanied by Lords Vruntled and Pacatore, both apparently unarmed but with a newly-found confidence that affords them far more protection than any armour.

Lord Vruntled steps forward. 'It wasn't Hector's idea. I was there when Vlast gave the order.' He turns to address Adib, 'Vlast was furious how you defended the dragons, arguing their case. He said you needed teaching a lesson.'

'Their bodies had bite marks...'

As Adib turns the metal jaw over the others watch him closely. He sees that their stories all lead to one conclusion – it wasn't the dragons who killed his family. Azi-Dhaka enters and crouches on one knee to examine the contraption. He looks up into Adib's face and the two men concur, silently.

'So are you with us?' Jonas asks. He holds out his fist, followed by Lord Vruntled and Lord Pacatore, then all three warriors

Jonas's eyes search their faces. 'We need to protect the one who can save us from the wrongdoings of poor Vlast.'

'Poor Vlast!' splutters Adib.

'Aye. The misguided fool has been trying to destroy anything he is afraid of – and when you head down that path there is no end. Nor joy,' Jonas adds as he leads the men outside. He watches Adib closely, as the sunlight shifts, spotlighting me as I stand, my hand on the great head of Astarot.

As Adib sees and recognises the great dragon for the first time he gives a roar that shakes the rafters of the timber house.

I wait silent as Astarot nods his head. Then as the great dragon speaks I translate, 'The dragons only wish for peace. The times when they killed were the times when they too were afraid, for mankind betrayed and slaughtered them too. I, Astarot, give thanks...'

I hesitate, finding it difficult to translate what comes next.

I glance at the great dragon who insists I translate every word.

"This young girl has taught me it is better to live differently. I thank her from the bottom of my heart for all she has done for me and my family and I would gladly give my life to help her – something I never thought I would say of a human. She has shown me more joy and pleasure in the family I had despised than I could ever have believed possible."

He turns to Adib, 'If she can do this for me – and I have lived millennia of hate and loathing – I am sure she can help you too.'

Adib snorts in disbelief, 'How can this child woman teach me? She is too young to understand.'

I leap to my feet, knocking the breakfast dishes aside.

'How can I? I will tell you how. I watched my mother killed before my very eyes – stabbed and kicked to death – by boots.'

My trembling finger points at Adib's boots – ancient boots made of dragon skin, that never wears out. In horror Adib's gaze moves from his boots to my face. I see the shock and disbelief.

'What was your mother's name, child?'

'What is that to you? I do not want to know if it was you and these boots that killed her – that would serve no purpose. For one thing that I do know is that the killing has to stop – any relief that revenge might bring is temporary.'

Adib stumbles forward and falls on his knees in the dirt, weeping. 'Oh child, woman, Azra. I have slain so many – both human and dragon – to avenge the death of my loved ones and it has been to no avail. I have felt so little relief, so little for all those lives.'

The great warrior sobs. His vast shoulders heaving. I take his great head in my hands and lift it from the tear-soaked earth.

I take his hand and put it on the dragon's nose. Man and dragon gaze into each other's eyes for a moment, and that moment is an eternity.

There is a reconciliation that shifts something, the shift moves the leaves in the trees, the birds stop singing in appreciation of the moment and the cat curls its tail around itself and sits statuesque on the porch.

Adib gazes into my face and I see the love for his wife and children as he throws his arms around me. The great warrior feels the shackles on his heart burst – and for the first time in years love comes in.

As the love radiates around Adib's tears dry up and he starts to laugh as love fills his heart for the first time in years. The laughter spreads, first me then Astarot, it spreads to Jonas, Rufus and the two lords and soon to all the warriors and for the forest rings with the sound of contentment, happiness and companionship.

Unbewitching Merilin

I, Samardashee felt strangely energised as Azra left for the City.

Her tales of Scotland – impossible for my mind to grasp at first – moved me. As I watched her ride off on the great Caledonian dragon my heart jumped in a way that made me gasp – I have never felt this emotion before.

'Is this what they call Love?' I ask myself.

Since my father's death I have felt fueled with anger and revenge. Vlast's destruction of Telus helped me maintain my rage. But the sight of the surface and daylight and the White Folk seeing the sun set for the first time, moved me. I knew I could not go on with this rage inside me. It felt too much.

So when I looked once more at the wasted remains of the underground city of Telus in the depths of the volcano, I see an opportunity.

Inspired, I go to the White Folk.

'Friends,' I say, and the initial surprise at me, the young arrogant Prince who has so recently been demanding and commanding them silences them and they turn to listen.

'I call you Friends because in my time of greatest need and despair you helped me.'

The White Folk nod first one or two, then they nod in agreement to each other, a silent acknowledgement that I am their friend. We stood together, helped each other, and I led them to safety. We have proved our friendship.

'Some have talked of going back to rebuild Telus, but looking around, at how you all see this new world of light, I say this is an opportunity, an opportunity for the White Folk to come and live in the light.'

'How can we, when Vlast will return at any moment to destroy us?'

'He may do that whether or not you are above or below ground. I would like to work together with the White Folk and build exactly where you want to live – and if that is here, above ground, in the sunlight then let us do that.'

'What about the job in hand? We are at war with Vlast.'

'Vlast is afraid. If we can show him that we want to work with him, that he has nothing to be afraid of, then I am sure he will let us build a new Telus where we choose.'

'Says the king whom Vlast has usurped!' exclaims a Telean.

'You don't just step into a new kingdom with us like that! You don't even know that we are not White Folk! We are Teleans,' exclaims another.

'I have no interest in being king,' I say, surprising even myself.

A snort of derision greets this.

'It is true,' I try to explain, 'All my life I have been brought up with that expectation, but now I see that I enjoy the freedom of not being king, of not needing to be responsible.'

'Then why are you taking responsibility now.'

This makes me laugh, I hold my hands up in surrender, 'You are right! I had not seen it. These are decisions for you and your people to make. I need to look after my own affairs.'

I withdraw and Cinaed comes to me. This wonderful dragon still makes me gasp in amazement whenever I see him. All my life I've been called the Dragon Slayer Prince and brought up to hate – and fear – these creatures. Yet now here I am, bond-father to this New Age Dragon.

He talks urgently to me, but the few sentences of Draco that I have learnt are not enough. Bond-father I may be, but I have not the Dragon Keepers innate knowledge of Draco, I have to learn the tongue.

'I wish I could understand you, friend.' I tell him.

Cinaed nudges me toward the edge of the volcano, urging him to look down into it. As he does so my head clears of all the images and thoughts of Telus and the Teleans. I am looking down at the crystals that line the volcanic plug. The ruby within my eye throbs and pulsates, but I move beyond the idea of it being painful and like a great ray of light the ruby begins to glow. Its rays fan out from my forehead, a beam of light that enables me and me alone to see through the walls of the volcano.

Suddenly I can see Merilin. My heart skips with joy to see her, this great warrior hunter, still alive. I watch as she is making her way through the maze of passageways. Then, separated by a mere few feet of rock I see Murray the Sea-Warrior running. I cry out to them, but their names echo hollow in the vast space of the volcanic plug. If they were to reach out through the few inches of the plug wall they are a mere arm's length apart.

Just as they are not aware of how close they are to each other they are unaware that I can see them with this new gift from the Ruby.

'Come,' I tell Cinaed and the dragon willingly lets me mount onto his back, for although the dragon has not my vision he has a dragon's instinct. The bond between dragon and bond-father means that Cinaed will do whatever I will – as long as it does not conflict with his dragon instinct.

In the moment before we leap into the abyss I glance over to the Teleans, who are now deep in debate. I feel a great sense of freedom and relief as we plunge into the nothingness. My stomach lurches, then the thrill of the adventure spurs me on.

From above the path to Merilin is clear, but alas, my vision is not a constant and while I have moments of clarity and the ability to see through dense matter that ability does not enable me to pass through the walls. We have to make our way through the tunnels.

But I am guided by the memory of my vision – of Merilin alive and Murray running.

I sense we are getting near to her, then suddenly Cinaed stops.

He stops and refuses to move. He gouges his ear with a claw and takes out a great wad of dragon earwax and gives it to me. All he says is what I think is 'ears'. I have no idea what he wants me to do. At last, frustrated he cuffs my ears with his great hand.

He tries to put it in my ear.

'No way,' I yell and hurl it on the ground.

He blocks the passageway and gives a snort, shooting a fireball at my feet. He roars and picks the earwax up on his tongue and holds it out for me.

There is no swaying this dragon.

'Is this to protect me?' I manage in Draco.

He nods.

'Okay.' I look at the disgusting yellow globule in my hand. If I'm going to do this I need to get over the feeling of disgust. I reach for my leather water flask on my belt and pour water over the stuff washing the dragon's sticky saliva off it. Suddenly it's glistening and golden. "Okay, let's do this.' I tell myself. Cinaed rolls his eyes in despair.

'Dragon saliva is a step too far,' I tell him.

Reluctantly I work the wax into two balls and put one in each ear. Cinaed nods, satisfied and stands aside to let me through.

It feels strange to have no sense of the sound of the cave and now that all is silent I realise there had been a sound, quite a pleasant pulsing vibration coming through the wall. Now that is gone. Also gone were the sounds that gave me a sense of place, the sense of how enclosed the tunnel is, the sound of water in the distance – all that is gone to me now.

I walk steadily for some time, until I begin to wonder if I have made a mistake, surely we should have caught up with Merilin by now? She was walking, wandering more like, gazing at the walls. There was no urgency in her movements and we had been moving quite swiftly.

Then we turn a corner – and she is there!

But this isn't the Merilin I know, the focused eager tracker, Merilin the Hunter. This woman is wandering around the tunnel smiling, gazing for moments at each rock or stone, any plant or fern. I call out her name – but she shows no sign of hearing me.

Worse still, when I stand in front of her she cannot see me!

I wave my hand in front of her face and her eyes don't change focus or blink.

I turn to Cinaed in concern, but Cinaed is busy extracting more wax from his ear.

'I wish you wouldn't do that,' I tell him.

But I might have known. He indicates I need to put the wax in Merilin's ears.

I follow her, unable to attract her attention, through the maze of tunnels within the volcano. She plays as if with unseen creatures, laughing, talking, dancing with them. I see her hold out her hands as if being held by some strange spirits who entice her, laughing and protesting into the water. Merilin is enchanted.

I take the wax from Cinaed. But deciding to do put dragon's wax into Merilin's ears and to actually do it are two different things. I'm scrambling around the rocks after her as she emerges from the water, slipping and sliding. She may not be able to see us, but something seems to magically guide her this way and that out of our path. It is only when she falls and lies laughing helplessly that I have a chance. I dive on top of her pinning her to the ground and put the wax in her ears.

She stops laughing abruptly as if waking up. She sees me for the first time.

'King Samardashee!' Even I can lip read that!

She looks shocked to find her king astride her.

Cautiously I get up, still holding her down by her shoulders. We are shouting unheard questions at each other.

She looks at her surroundings, puzzled.

Then she begins to poke at her ear. I stop her.

Cinaed flies us farther on through the tunnels then stops and indicates we can remove the wax. Instantly we bombard each other with questions. She stops, and I tell her.

'You were enchanted, I think. At least that's my guess. You couldn't see us until I put...' I hesitate reluctant to tell her at first what I've done, 'I put dragon wax in your ears and it seems to have worked.'

Then there is a flicker of remembrance and she says, 'I was having such fun, I seem to remember. Oh, King Samardashee, why don't we go back and join them for a while?' she says eagerly.

'I don't think that's a good idea, besides, I'm not King any more. Vlast has been crowned king.'

This galvanizes Merilin and all yearning for the ethereal song stops as she leaps into action.

'Then we must overthrow him,' she says scrambling to her feet.

'I don't want a war just to put me on a throne.'

'What has happened to you while I've been away?' Merilin asks.

'I've been spending more time with people,' I tell her, 'and it's very different to spending time in court.'

She steps back and looks at me. 'So, what now?'

'We need to find Murray. He isn't far away.' I tell her.

'That's it?'

'For now. We need to take one step at a time.'

Merilin scents the air. 'This way,' she says and we head off.

Cinaed insists we put the dragon wax in again and as he seems to know which tunnels are filled with the sound of enchantment and which are not. We agree.

213

Murray the Sea Warrior

Cinaed flies low through the passages, his wings tucked in at his sides. I hadn't believed him when he said he could do this, I had visions of us dive bombing onto the ground. But a dragon would surely know how to fly better than I so here we are this streamlined Dragon speeding through the tunnels, the airstream pinning me close to his back.

We had to lie low along the dragon's back – once Merilin raised her head and the movement caused Cinaed to veer and swear in *Draco*. I can hear him speak in *Draco* and check that my ears are still plugged, they are and this is how I learn that *Draco* can be heard *through* the Dragon wax.

We follow Murray from above, even the great dragon struggling to match the fleet-footed warrior's speed.

Murray runs through the passages – at first we thought he was fleeing from something, but there is no urgency in him and he never looks back, occasionally he slows and stops a moment as if to take in his surroundings - but never long enough for us to catch up.

We know this must be an enchantment because of the speed.

'He's running for the sheer pleasure of it!' I yell in a clunky *Draco* and Settler. 'Well I'm glad he's enjoying it,' I complain under my breath, 'It's not my idea of fun.'

So Murray keeps on the running – and keeps on running, running, running.

The underground animals join in, following him until he has a great host of creatures crawling, scurrying, flying with him. They befriend him – the birds bring him tasty snacks of the green foliage growing on the cave walls. At first he is reluctant to eat, but they hover around his mouth with them, until he eats. Soon he doesn't need to stop, for they feed him on the run. He satisfies his thirst from the clear waterfalls that flow down the cave walls, he barely needs to stop to drink from them.

'I don't think we can catch him,' I observe to myself. 'This looks like a casual pace to him and we are struggling to keep up with it.'

By now Murray has a happy chattering crowd accompanying him as he runs deeper and deeper into the volcano.

'We need to find a short cut, a way to head him off,' I try to tell Cinaed as he pauses to drink.

I hold onto Cinaed with my knees and cup my hands to drink from the waterfall. I see my reflection in the water in my hands. The ruby pulsates in my forehead and the reflection turns the water red – but this doesn't feel like a danger warning. This is clarity. The ruby reveals within my hands the caves mapped out and the tiny figure of Murray, running. I feel a real appreciation for the ruby as the map fades and then I gulp the water down.

'This way!' I tell Cinaed and instinctively he knows I know the way and lets me direct him through the maze of passages to a narrow pass where we wait.

'Have we missed him?' I wonder.

Then we hear the commotion of birds and animals and Murray appears, halted by the bulk of Cinaed in the passageway.

217

For a moment I think that Murray recognises me, then I see his eyes, like Merilin's earlier, are not in this world. Murray makes to clamber over Cinaed to continue on his way. Cinaed's roar at this insult reverberates through the cave and a warning bolt of fire causes Murray to fall onto his backside.

I seize my chance and take the shocked Murray by the shoulders and plug his ears with dragon wax. He grips my hand and notices my father's ring on my little finger and utters one word and I can read it plain upon his lips.

'Sire?' he says, the word dredged deep from within his memory. I am about to deny it but dread the warrior falling back into the oblivion of his entrancement. It's easier to nod, 'Aye, King Samardashee.'

The ingrained training of the warrior kicks in and Murray falls to his knees, 'At your service, Sire.'

'Well at least someone thinks you are King,' remarks Cinaed.

'Now let's get out of here,' I urge and the dragon flies us deep into the heart of the volcano.

Into the Pit, Death and Transformation

We set off. Silas Jonas and Lords Vruntled and Pacatore with the great warriors Azi-Dhaka, Adib and Baligh, retracing the journey Constance and I made all those months ago from the Forest of Discontent to the bottom of the abyss. Only this time I am not a prisoner, I am leading the warriors.

I remember this as if it was another girl who had done this. It feels now as if back then I was a mere child carrying the newly hatched Cinaed in my backpack. Now I am the hunter, searching for the missing warriors.

We find a pair of boots, warrior's boots, unlike Adib's these are soft, made from young, soft dragon skin, supple and shaped to the foot, hand tooled with pictures of animals, running deer and wolves.

Adib picks them up and knows at a glance whose they are. 'Merilin's,' he tells us. Beside them are bare footprints in the mud that appear to disappear into the cave wall. While we are puzzling at this the sound of laughter comes to us, a sound that soon becomes singing, an ethereal sound. The voices sound like running water and stars twinkling, that conjure up images for Adib of being embraced of being loved, for me they remind me of running and laughing into my father's arms, a feeling of such joy at being swung up onto my mother's horse to sit nestled safely behind her.

'Stop your ears,' Granpa commands. He turns to Rufus who hands them some precious dragon wax from his pack.

'Where might you have got this?' Adib asks him.

Rufus smiles, 'All kinds pass through the forest and when you treat them well it is amazing what gifts you may receive.

Adib nods in approval and the men all know what to do – they start to insert the wax into their ears. I take the wax reluctantly. I pause, I want to hear more. Granpa makes as if to take the wax from me and insert it into my ears himself.

'Wait! I tell him. 'This is beautiful singing, Granpa. Why would you not want to hear it?'

His face contorts with pain. 'Those voices are the spirits in the caves who entice humans into their world to join in their revels and keep them there. They remind me of what I've lost.'

'Is that a bad thing?' I ask him, confused. I stop his hand a moment from placing the wax in his other ear.

Tears fall from Granpa's eyes as he shakes his head, 'I do not know any more, lass.'

'Their song is offering laughter, joy and happiness to me – maybe they will to you too.'

'It's an illusion!' Adib has removed the wax from one of his ears to warn me.

'Then we must remind ourselves to wake up. But if this is what happened to Merilin then we need to go after her.'

Adib holds me back by my arm. 'If we go into this other world there may be no coming back.'

'I am ready to go. Are you?'

Adib grunts 'Ha! I never thought I'd be faced down by a young...'

'What? Girl? My gender isn't the issue, it's learning to decide what you really want in life. This sounds good to me.'

I tilt my head to listen some more. Slowly Adib removes the second piece of wax. The others watch him carefully and follow suit.

As we allow the music to flow into our very beings the cave begins to change. The wall in front of us becomes a great waterfall.

Then Adib bids us stop.'We must bring Ochamore with us. We cannot leave him alone back there.'

We turn and see the entrance to the passage way that I oh so long ago walked down with the newly hatched dragon that is now Ceonid in my backpack.'

Granpa takes charge, 'This is clear, Adib and Azi-Dhaka need to go and bring Ochamore back while we go ahead and track Merilin.

The two warriors set off for their comrade while we retrace our steps into the passageway where we once more hear faint music.

Merilin's footprints continue, so we follow the trail along the passage and there is a shimmering that divides the dark passage from another world, and the beautiful world with the great waterfall comes more and more into focus..

I have the feeling that there is someone walking beside me. I keep stopping to check, but it's always just a glimpse of something not quite real out of the corner of my eye.

Beneath our feet is soft moss and a delicate light illuminates our way. We move towards the singing.

Suddenly I turn and see that Astarot has stopped. I beckon him – and with his dragon eyes he can see into the world I have entered.

'What is it?' I ask.

When I look into the great dragon's eyes I see that he is afraid. 'What are you afraid of?'

'That I am not worthy of what they promise.'

'You understand their song?'

He nods. 'I have done so much wrong, Azra. They are promising that *all* will feel joy and happiness and love. I do not deserve that.'

'Others are prepared to forgive but first you must forgive yourself. Come, what is the worst that can happen?'

The great creature shudders. 'I have been close to death many times and not been afraid, but now I feel it is closer at hand than ever I have experienced and that it is not the ending that I was hoping for, but a beginning. I am more afraid of these sweet fairy promises than of all the warriors I have ever slain or encountered.'

'So wait here and we will return for you.'

This shakes his dragon pride. He draws himself up to his full height. 'No, young Azra, I promised to escort you and I will, my fear is nothing compared to the honour you do me letting me accompany you.'

Our group of warriors – for now I think of Granpa and even the Lords Vruntled and Pacatore as such, are waiting patiently. They have seen the exchange between the great dragon and me, and gaze in awe at the creature as he appears to have doubled in size.

'That was a great thing you did for him,' Granpa tells me and I remember he is a Dragoman, he has learned *Draco*.

'Me? I did nothing. It was all him, he has faced his fear,' I tell him.

Granpa shakes his head, 'It was much more than that, he chose to feel better, you inspired him in the way that you have inspired us all.' Granpa looks around at the group.

Their faces glow in the light for their courage comes from within with the ease and strength of inspired men with a purpose.

'They do, don't they? I feel I'm on an adventure that just gets better and better.

This is a beautiful place and the singing is the sweetest thing that I have ever heard.'

Granpa looks around him and sees the light catching on the waterfall creating rainbows as it cascades into the pool below. The singing hovers in this beautiful place and orbs of light dart across the water, inviting. I laugh with delight and strip off my boots and heavy outer garb and dive into the pool.

As I swim the dust and cares of the past weeks wash away. I dive deeper, and in the clear water find myself swimming alongside golden fish that leap over me in apparent delight at their new playmate. My laughter is so infectious that soon all relax and cast aside their weapons to drink from the fresh water. Lord Pacatore and Granpa even join me in the water with pantaloons rolled up above their knees.

Astarot waits until they finish before he drinks. His thirst so great that the water level drops, revealing a set of stepping stones that wind down through the cavern wall.

I wring out my hair tying it back with a piece of vine from the abundance of foliage growing all around us.

The mood has lightened and changed from the determined band who stepped into this world, they have been infected with the sound of enchantment and I feel a lightness of spirit that I have never known before.

We follow the singing orbs – that we all can now glimpse sight of out of the corners of our eyes. They lead us to a place where we can see the young dragons with Constance and a group of the White Folk.

I call out, delighted. Alas – they cannot hear me yet their conversation drifts through to us.

'You must believe me,' Constance is imploring them; 'Vlast was planning to poison the water.'

The young dragons ruffle their wings in disdain, 'The White Folk have drunk of it and it did no harm to them.'

'...Because the poison only kills dragons!' Constance cries.

The young dragons are dehydrated; I can see that, the colour has faded from their scales. Dragons such as Astarot can go for weeks if need be without water, however the young need to be fed and especially watered frequently and regularly.

The cheekiest and boldest dragon is at the water's edge. 'I do not trust you woman, for you were the friend of Vlast, you saved his life – I do not believe you are doing this to save us but to watch us die slowly from lack of sustenance.'

As he says this he reaches out his long neck to drink...

'NO!' The scream rips through the two worlds as Astarot bursts through the shimmering wall. 'STOP!'

The outburst has made the young dragon pause but he looks at Astarot in disdain.

'What old one? You take her side too. Well I will make my own decision.'

His head lowers to the pool but Astarot knocks him aside with a blow – and to Constance and to my horror – drinks. He drinks so deep that the pool is almost emptied.

'Hah! Greedy one!' the young dragon is turning in fury on the old dragon but before he can touch Astarot the old dragon keels over.

The White Folk and Constance stand stunned at the appearance of Astarot.

As I step through the barrier between the two worlds its edges shimmer revealing the portal.

I kneel beside the great dragon wrapping my arms around his neck. He is still warm.

'He can't be dead,' tears rolling down my cheeks. 'This is all my fault.'

'How can this be your fault?' a voice says.

I look up to see – Samardashee.

'*The Handbook* warned us and I ignored it, I persuaded him to come. There should never be more than four dragons in Set. That is why we left the Raptor Dragons to guard the perimeter.'

'It was Astarot's choice to come with you.' Granpa reminds me, gently.

'He was the oldest dragon on earth – the only one left from the Great Age from when the planet was formed – he is...' I correct myself, gulping for breath, 'he was as old as the earth, formed from the stuff that the stars are made of.'

I feel disembodied as if hearing words coming from someone else.

The young dragon snorts in disbelief, 'Is that what he told you?'

'No, it was in *The Handbook*. But once I knew that I started to ask him questions.'

I stroke his old grey lifeless form.

'I wish I had asked him more. He knew so much, so much.'

Samardashee has his hand on the old dragon's scaly heart. The glow has died out, but as he feels his love and respect for the old dragon the ruby shard in his own heart begins to pulse and glow.

In Azi-Dhaka too the shard begins to pulse and shine and where his hand touches the dragon's scales begin to glow, as if a light is shining through the old grey scales of the ancient dragon.

Constance and I exchange a look.

'I've heard tell of crystals transforming the dead.' Constance tells me. 'But there are only three parts of the ruby here.'

Baligh whispers his eloquent words into the dragon's ear tracing their ruby lifeline into his brain. The words spark lights around his neural pathways, revealing the road map of this dragon's brain: 'Come old one, there is more, much more in your life yet. It is not yet your time to leave this plane. Come rejoin us.'

The dragon seems to have the life force flowing through him, but the movement is still deep within him. We watch the ripple of ruby light spreading throughout his body, a tremor so imperceptible that when it stops I wonder if I imagined it. But it happens again, a pulsing wave within the grey carcass.

Then slowly the vast grey jaws fall open – and a creature emerges.

The dull grey skin that was once Astarot is cast aside to reveal a bright green creature – the green of emeralds, with body markings that glisten like pure gold. As one we step back in astonishment and wonder. This magnificent beast – far larger, far more magnificent than Astarot – gives off a brightness that is almost blinding.

It dwarfs the young dragons, making them look like mere pups compared to this mythical beast.

Physically Astarot had been big, far bigger than Cinaed and any of the newborn, but his old weary way made him seem much smaller, so the shock of this transformation is all the greater.

All eyes are on the newly emerged creature. 'What is this?' Samardashee exclaims in wonder.

'This is what was Astarot,' replies the creature who turns his unseeing eye towards Samardashee.

Constance places a hand on Samardashee's arm – 'His transformation is incomplete for only three of the seven parts of the ruby are present.'

'Adib and Azi-Dhaka have gone for Ochamore...' There is a pause as all realize that for Ochamore there is no reprieve, no second chance.

'There is no time,' Constance states, 'We cannot wait. We will what we can with what we have.'

The blind creature flails around trying to get its bearings from our voices and then lies exhausted on the ground.

'Hush. Be still.' Constance tells it. She indicates for him to put his hand on the creature's third eye. Nothing happens. Samardashee removes his hand but I take it and replace it on in the centre of the creature's head.

'You have to help him, your strength is in your far-reaching sight, help him,' I urge. Still nothing happens.

I stand on tiptoe to reach Samardashee's ear. 'You have to believe.'

He sheds a single tear and the ruby teardrop rolls down his cheek and falls, dropping as purposefully as if he had placed it with an eye-dropper, onto the creature's unseeing third eye. The drop spreads, dissolving the papery tissue as if unwrapping a gift, revealing a multifaceted eye that mirrors us all a thousand-fold, mirrors us and sees beyond us, seeing into all the worlds in the cave and beyond. The sight stuns us and we step back in amazement and disbelief.

The creature moves its wings and flutters, but its legs are lifeless. Murray steps up and takes them in his hands, massaging each in turn and he is bathed in the ruby glow emanating from the shard in his leg that envelops them both, invigorating and quickening the creature's limbs.

'Watch out!' Lord Pacatore exclaims.
Constance turns to him, 'He is transformed.'
The creature hovers in mid-air before us. It's translucent, with wings twice the size of its body. Its great tail suddenly whips around itself as it pulls it's wings in, making itself small, and then unfurls its tail and wings and flaps them, creating a breeze that makes Samardashee's hair and my cloak billow out behind us.
'This bears as much relation to a dragon as...' Constance searches for a comparison, '...a butterfly does to a caterpillar.'
We have been so busy watching the creature that we haven't noticed Astarot's shed skin.
'Look!' I tell them and point at the disappearing skin.

As one they glance down to see it is already almost crumbled away to dust.

'Well, one thing's for sure,' Samardashee says. 'That creature will be no good in a battle.'

The warriors nod in agreement.

As they do they hear laughter, a deep, echoing laughter that takes them a moment to realise where it is coming from.

'Was that you, Astarot?' I ask.

Amid the laughter a 'Yes' sounds out as the exuberant giddy creature loops and flies in ecstatic circles around the cavern.

'He doesn't look much like a Prince of Hell now!' Baligh exclaims.

'Why do you say that?' I ask.

'That's what his name means *Astarot, Prince of Hell.*'

'He's so beautiful.'

Astarot hovers mid-air. 'Beautiful?'

'I don't know about that, but I do feel the life force – I feel young again.'

'Yes, you're beautiful.' I tell him.

He tries to do a loop and crashes. His flight is erratic.

'What's wrong with him?'

'His incomplete, he needs his sense of touch to fly. He needs the other shards.'

Constance looks concerned and we watch as the creature weaves around drunkenly.

He looks at his reflection in the remnants of the pool and swoops closer to check that it is him. 'That's me?'

The three warriors all roar with laughter at the disbelief in the creature's voice.

'I think you need a new name.' Constance says.

We look at each other blankly. This creature is so unlike the dusty old dragon that brought me back here it's difficult to come up with one.

'*Parvaneh*,' says one.

'What does that mean?' I ask.

'Butterfly.'

I am nodding in agreement but Cinaed shakes his head.

'No, no – a woman's name doesn't fit. It's too delicate. This creature has strength.'

A voice breaks through the discussion echoing around the cavern.

'*My name is Khepra*' the creature tells us.

'But…are you still Astarot in there?' I ask him urgently.

'I am and I am not. What I was is finished what I have become I am. I Became and the Becoming became.'

'Well I'm glad that's cleared that up,' says Lord Pacatore.

The Dragon Keeper's Handbook suddenly bursts out of my backpack.

'Always the one for a dramatic entrance,' I tell it. This time it's in the shape of an ancient scroll.

Carefully I unfold it and read from it:

The Dragon Keeper's Handbook
This is the record of the Great Priest King whose utterance of the Word brought the very gods into existence.

My hands start trembling as I read. I notice Granpa looking at me, concerned, 'This is unsettling you child. Put it away.'

I shake my head, 'No. I need to do this. This is important.'

I shift my feet to balance myself more strongly and adjust the book in my hands. Clearing my throat, I continue:

When the Seven are assembled then order will be restored and time will be no more. When All are One then Magic will be the Power in the world and Force will be overcome as Mystery takes its place.

Mystery is a Strange Attractor and when this replaces Force and the Power of Light returns to the World then the portal in the

Halls of Amenti will be accessible to humankind.

'What does it mean?' I ask.

Khepra rolls his head, easing his neck. 'When we came back in time, that was the portal. The portal was sealed at the time of the Pharaohs to avoid anyone with ill-intention from mis-using it.'

'So why has it opened again?'

'That is what I have been pondering.'

'The explosion?' suggests Samardashee.

'Possibly – but the magic used to seal it should have withstood that...' the beautiful creature pauses. 'There is a legend – *The Legend of the Serpent.*'

He looks at me, his multi-faceted eye reflecting the myriad images of me.

Granpa and the Warriors all turn their gaze on me.

I shift uncomfortably at all this attention. 'What?' I ask.

'Old wives tales,' snorts Lord Vruntled.

Constance turns on him sharply, 'And most of the wisdom of the world is contained in those tales'

'True,' nods Khepra in placatory tones.

'So what is *The Legend of the Serpent*?' I ask.

'This is not the time or the place,' Granpa tells me.

'He is right,' interrupts Samardashee stepping forward.

Granpa Jonas has moved close to the divide between this world and the waterfall world we came through. He beckons Samardashee who gazes with his ruby eye.

'I see them!' he declares and he tries in vain to pass through. 'They cannot hear me.'

Baligh calls out, 'Adib! Azi-Dhaka!'

Then Samardashee exclaims, they hear you!'

'This way, follow my voice…'

And before his sentence is complete the two warriors burst through with Ochamore carried on two spears between them.

'Come, quickly,' Constance calls, before they can greet each other.

Her reason for urgency is clear when we come close for Khepra is lying his wings lifeless and his eyes dull.

Constance places Ochamore's lifeless body alongside Khepra and unwraps Ochamore's hand. It too is dull, lifeless. Yet as the others gather round the ruby shards start to glow within each one of them and with a faint yet distinct hum so does the shard in Ochamore's hand.

I find I'm counting my breath in the eternity of silence as we wait, for what?

For the movement in Khepra's abdomen as it fills with air, for the fluttering of wings as the life force flows through them once more, for the light in his multi-faceted crystalline eyes that mirror our focused faces.

It's as if we all breathe as one, a communal sigh of relief as he returns to life. Then Khepra is flying around as if nothing had ever happened.

Samardashee is standing beside me and I catch sight of the beaming smile that reaches from ear to ear as he watches the joy and delight of Khepra's flight. Then he turns to me,

'We need to decide our plan of action.'

I look around at our surroundings – the beautiful waterfall cascading thousands of feet creates rainbows that colour the cave walls. The whole is bathed in a golden light. I turn to Samardashee, 'Here is good.'

'What do you mean?' he asks.

'This looks like a great place to live,' I tell him.

'We wouldn't be safe here from Vlast and his men,' he replies.

Constance steps forward, 'Azra is right. This is a good place, and Vlast thinks he has entombed us all and poisoned the dragons through the water supply. To him we are dead.'

'We cannot just submit to Vlast!' Adib cries out.

'We are not,' I tell him, 'We are creating a new world. At this point we have a choice – to reveal to Vlast that we are alive and continue the fighting. The alternative is to create our new home here… '

I open my arms to allow them time to take in the beauty of their surroundings. Fish are leaping in the pool far below us, exotic birds fly around our heads. Azi-Dhaka takes his sword and cuts a great fruit that he slices in half and tosses one half to Adib who barely hesitates before sinking his teeth into the succulent flesh – his great grin of satisfaction is enough to show his consent.

Murray is still not sure. 'What if this too isn't real? You are proposing that we live underground away from the sun and the sea...'

Khepra interrupts him, 'This is also a portal to Scotland and the rest of the Earth.'

'Scotland? Scotland? Scotland!' Murray murmurs as he realises that all his dreams have been delivered at once.

'We aren't prisoners – if anyone is it is Vlast cut off from the rest of the world who is,' Constance declares.

Murray takes me by the arm and swings me round, then picks up Constance by the waist, lifts her off the ground and twirls her round as she screams with delight and excitement. The cry of Scotland echoes around the cave and the others take it up in delight. Merilin brings out her flute and plays a reel and we all dance – celebrating the New Land we have found that seems to be welcoming us in.

'Oh Granpa,' I laugh, breathless. 'Things just get better and better!'

'They do, Azra, indeed they do.'

Characters

Agraciana – meaning, forgiveness. Daughter of Astarot and Gloriana; dragon mother of Regnatha

Arnbjorg – sister to Balder and heiress to the Icelandic Kingdom

Astarot – the Dragon Emperor of Alba and the Ice Lands.

Balder – Dragon prince from Iceland claw fasted to Regnatha

Cinaed – firstborn of the new dragons in Set, bonded to Samardashee

Dybra – one of the White Folk, a healer who accompanies Constance in her search for the ruby.

Gertrude – Vlast's wife.

Gloriana – Astarot's wife, mother of Agraciana and Regnatha's grandmother.

Hector – Vlast's henchman

Khepra – meaning 'creator, the rising sun' is the name given to Astareot on his transformation

MacOolafur – the name Astarot bestows on his sons, meaning son of the heir of the ancestors combining their Scots and Icelandic heritage.

Rak – son and firstborn of Astarot and Gloriana

Regnatha – aka Reggie the dragon bonded at birth to Azra

The Seven Warriors

Adib - the Wolf - the ruby shard goes into his heart

Azi -Dhaka - Dragon Slayer the ruby shard goes into his skin

Baligh the Eloquent formerly The Stutterer - the ruby shard goes into his tongue

Merilin - the Hunter - the ruby shard goes into her nose

Murray - the Sea Warrior – the ruby goes into his heel making him fleet of foot and tireless

Ochamore – the fiercest warrior – the ruby shard goes into his hand

Samardashee - *the boy king* - the ruby shard goes into his third eye

Glossary

Alaxsxaq – the volcanic lands where Astarot's parents retired to.

Albion – the oldest known name for the island of Great Britain:

Alba (Scottish Gaelic) Albain (Irish) Nalbin (Manx) Alban (Welsh, Cornish, Breton). Latinised as Albania, Anglicised as Albany – once alternative names for Scotland. From the Welsh Alb-ien earthworld OR Albho – proto-European

meaning white (cliffs of Dover) OR alb –
Proto-IndoEuropean meaning hill

anallpòg – breathkiss a sign of close
affection when a dragon gives a light fiery
kiss, using their heartfire rather than their
lips
dràgon chridhe – dragon heart

draki – the language, both spoken and
pictorial, of dragons

drakiafi – dragon grandfather (from the
Icelandic)

drakiamma – dragon grandmother (from
the Icelandic)

drakiathair – dragon father

drakibanrigh – dragon queen

drakiabarnabarn –dragon granddaughter

drakibràthair-màthair – dragon uncle on mother's side

drakiflath – dragon prince

drakimhac – dragon son singular

drakimathair – dragon mother

drakinighean-peathar – dragon niece (sororal, sister's daughter)

maethair – mother

mega- annia – a period of time of millions of years

saedraki – sea-dragon

starward – after a dragon has completed its purpose it transforms by disintegrating into almost pure energy, ascending to the heavens and becomes a star constellation.

Astarot's mother and father when they united the Northern territories through their pure love became the constellation Draco

Suidh Artair – Arthur's Seat Draki Cridhe – a.k.a. Alba Dragonheart of Alba

Telus – the underground city of the White Folk

Thanks

This second book is a very well-travelled one. With thanks to Michael and Mishka Barnett whose home and community in Germany helped grow the roots of this. Ken Hay whose friendship and meetings in Edinburgh helped shape this into book form. The inspirational friendship, walks and meals in the beautiful Edinburgh home of Tarimo Madir Mabbott. The friendship, enthusiasm and proof reading skills of Louise Cardon; the support of Sian-Elin Flint-Freel; the inspiration of Esther Hicks and her Abraham-Hicks workshops and their encouragement to edit.

To all the Simply Sisterhood and other sisters who have encouraged and supported me; to all those brothers, both blood-brothers and in spirit,

who have helped me grow and say what I mean
and mean what I want to say.

Coming Soon Book 3 in 'The Fire and the Flame Series' 'The Eye of the Serpent.'

Printed in Poland
by Amazon Fulfillment
Poland Sp. z o.o., Wrocław